What if the believers  enforcement, anti-ter gence were also empo God, spiritual giftings, ...u uivine intervention through Presence, prayer, and being led by the Spirit in dreams and visions?

What would happen in world events if we walked in Christ as He would with the Father? If we stood in our placement (1 John 4:17) and acted in concert with a higher realm?

J.L. McKay takes the lid off that possibility and opens up a space where we can imagine the intentionality of Heaven entering the complexities of the modern world and bringing light, truth, and the power of divine intervention. We are all children of light called to be soldiers and warriors of dynamic purpose.

The Overcomers is the account of an elite anti-terrorism task force, the O.T.F, and their battle to prevent an internet breach of worldwide government systems that would also destroy a natural gas production facility destined to release billions of dollars into the Israeli economy.

I admired the single-minded intentionality of the O.T.F and their commitment to the values of their lifestyle in Christ regardless of circumstances. Their honor and devotion to God, one another, and their cause is a revelation of the realities of a heaven to earth spirituality.

These are not just protagonists in the quest for freedom with security; they are also carriers of the Presence who partner with goodness to create outcomes unforeseen in the shadowy world of the hostilities between good and evil. It is also the narrative of what is possible in the everyday story of your life and mine in Christ. It tells us who we can become in this cosmic battle.

History, tradition, revelation, and truth are all

powerfully intertwined in a gripping tale that forces each of us to comprehend the potential effects of mixing spirituality, a heavenly mindset, and language from another realm with the wickedness, atrocity, and cruelty of the modern world.

To overcome is to exercise power. To walk in power we must know our identity. To embrace power and call things into being is the height of Godliness.

This is a new genre in the annals of the Intelligence Community that blends one unknown world with another more powerful, hidden realm that lies at the heart of the true conflict between the forces of goodness and malevolence.

More please!!

—AUTHOR AND SPEAKER GRAHAM COOKE

THE OVERCOMERS

J. L. McKAY

A NOVEL

Dive in and discover new worlds!

Jeannine

CREATION
HOUSE

THE OVERCOMERS by J. L. McKay
Published by Creation House
A Charisma Media Company
600 Rinehart Road
Lake Mary, Florida 32746
www.charismamedia.com

Unless otherwise noted, all Scripture quotations are from the Holy Bible, New International Version of the Bible. Copyright © 1973, 1978, 1984, International Bible Society. Used by permission

Design Director: Bill Johnson
Cover design by Nathan Morgan

Visit the author's website: www.theovercomer.com.

Library of Congress Cataloging-in-Publication Data:
2014937539

International Standard Book Number: 978-1-62136-746-8
E-book International Standard Book Number:
978-1-62136-747-5

While the author has made every effort to provide accurate telephone numbers and Internet addresses at the time of publication, neither the publisher nor the author assumes any responsibility for errors or for changes that occur after publication.

First edition

14 15 16 17 18 — 987654321
Printed in Canada

To him who overcomes, I will give some of the hidden manna. I will also give him a white stone with a new name written on it, known only to him who receives it.

—REVELATION 2:17

PROLOGUE
Tel Aviv, Israel

THE MEDITERRANEAN SKY, blue and clear before the explosion, was now filled with dust and smoke. Students from other parts of the campus were still running toward the Jewish Studies building. Where the staff offices lined the garden, a jagged hole had ruptured the concrete wall. The university wouldn't be holding classes today.

No one had approached the explosion site except one man. He was already inside. He stood in unmarked combat gear, legs planted in rubble and books, in what had been the office of Dr. Levi Uziel, professor of history. Light that once entered through a window now came in through what used to be the wall. The sun rays turned the swirling particles of dust into gold.

The man had a few minutes before the Israeli Security Agency (ISA) agents arrived. He looked at the professor's body flung back against a bookshelf, a paper still clasped in his left hand. It was a piece of that morning's Haaretz newspaper. The rest of its pages were scattered around the room. The man laid his hand on the professor's forehead and spent a moment speaking in a low, calm voice. He reached inside the man's collar and unfastened the leather cord tied to a white stone with faint veins of red. He put the necklace in his pocket.

The man unclasped Dr. Uziel's fingers to take the paper from them. A quick scan told him the professor had found something of interest. In the heading for an article on Yom Ha'atzmaut, Israel's Independence, the Hebrew letter ו—vav—was circled over and over.

A voice came from the doorway. "He was one of our contacts."

The ISA agent came to stand next to the man, who handed him the newspaper page and said, "This mean anything to you?"

The agent took the paper. "The letter? No. But he was one of the smartest people I knew. He probably had a reason he'll never be able to explain."

The agent looked at the paper and frowned. He shifted his gaze to the white stone pendant around the neck of the man standing in front of him.

The agent looked into the man's eyes: "You knew this one would happen, didn't you?"

The man looked down at the professor, whose eyes were still open, as if watching them.

"Yes. But not in time."

Chapter One
Fort Worth, Texas

THE NECKLACE WAS tightening around her throat, the white stone pendant choking her. She moved her head, trying to breathe.

"It's not mine!" she kept trying to say, but she couldn't catch her breath. Gasping, Ma'ayan sat up straight in bed.

It had been a dream. She wasn't wearing a necklace—the sheets had just twisted around her neck. She took a few deep breaths as her heart thudded loud enough to hear.

Wait, that wasn't her heart—what was that sound? Her pager.

She reached for it on the nightstand and looked at the number. "Of course."

Blinking away the sleep, she pulled on the jeans she'd already worn two days in a row. Outside her bedroom window, the spring sun was just beginning to shine through the pecan tree blossoms. If she had time, it would be lovely to sip coffee and watch the day begin. But she never had time.

In the bathroom, she splashed some water on her face, checking that she didn't have pillow marks deep across her cheek. She had never thought much about beauty, even though people had always told her she was beautiful, with her dramatic eyes, thick dark hair, and flawless olive complexion.

But that olive complexion was looking tired these days. Ma'ayan was starting to realize that forty-something skin required at least occasional care. Though she'd never been one to primp, she had found herself buying one of those facial creams in a package promising all sorts of rejuvenation.

She slapped on some of the cream and sighed. "I could use some mind, body, and spirit rejuvenation."

In the kitchen, her son was eating cereal and reading the box. Ma'ayan's heart leapt for the second time this morning. She remembered Eitan doing that when he was a boy. For a moment, she saw him at age seven instead of seventeen—dressing as Spiderman for Halloween, running across the yard on summer nights trying to catch lightning bugs, waving at her through the bus window. But the impressions faded quickly. Eitan was now taller than his father, though he hadn't seen Nathan since he came up to his chest.

Ma'ayan shifted her focus from her ex-husband back to her son, as she always tried to. Eitan's dark hair, inherited from her Israeli genes, was tousled with sleep.

"Morning, Mom."

She shook herself, remembering the pager and the morning ahead of her. "Morning, Eitan."

"Cereal?" he asked, picking up the box and waving it at her.

"No time, but thanks." Ma'ayan grabbed an apple and shoved it in her jacket pocket as she leaned over to kiss Eitan on the forehead.

He smiled. "Off to report on more death and destruction?"

"You know it. Have a great day at school. You'll ace that math test."

He groaned.

Before she reached the door to the garage, Eitan turned and asked, "Will you be home for dinner?"

"Yes. Your turn to cook, right?"

"Oh yeah. You'll be impressed."

"I always am, my chef. Always am. See you this evening."

Ma'ayan left through the hall into the garage. She hit the garage door opener and started her old Triumph.

Male bikers always looked when she rode, and she always ignored them. In fact, she had ignored men since Nathan had left her. After the first few years as a single mother, Ma'ayan had grown accustomed to her life and decided to not date men until Eitan left for college. The fact that he was graduating in less than two months was starting to bother her in more ways than one.

Once Ma'ayan was on the road, her bike beneath her and the wind loud in her helmet, she felt ready for her day. She'd spent years at the mercy of her pager while working as an investigative reporter assigned to the FBI SWAT and later with the Domestic Terrorism Task Force, the DTTF. Though she dreaded being jolted from sleep, she loved getting to see night skies and breaking dawns. Sometimes, the skies reminded her of Tel Aviv, and she would be transported from North Central Texas to her childhood home.

Ma'ayan wondered what she would encounter this morning. Recently, she'd been following a group similar to the DTTF. This one had the interesting name of Overcomer Task Force, or OTF. Of all the agencies she had reported on in the past, this one fascinated her the most. Though they had intensive training and bravery, the group was somehow different than any other she had worked with. If she had to name that difference, she'd probably call it honor—almost mystically so.

Though the OTF dealt with what Eitan called "death and destruction," they didn't get cynical or jaded. The agents fully supported their team members, not just in physical defense but relationally too. They also didn't seem to self-promote—a common practice among most any other organization Ma'ayan had worked with. But what struck her the most about the OTF agents was that they seemed to bless or pray over victims and perpetrators. This she could not understand—extending grace to the people who were responsible for terror—but it fascinated her nonetheless.

And Ma'ayan Bracha was no stranger to violence or danger. Unlike the OTF, she had grown a bit jaded. She certainly had zero compassion for terrorists. Early in her career, she had been invited to participate in operations of the federal government's DTTF. In the wake of incidents in Oklahoma City and at the Twin Towers, the U.S. government was looking for solutions to the rising dangers of terrorism within the borders of the United States. And although Ma'ayan was a civilian, an inexplicable favor with authorities had gained her entry where others were denied.

As she became a leading consultant to the media, Ma'ayan had developed a reputation for offering pointed insight and cogent answers to tough questions. She soon began to develop a presence on TV news magazines and political talk shows.

With her friendly and approachable personality, Ma'ayan became a familiar face in sound bites and headlines. But more than any other aspect of her job, Ma'ayan liked the feeling of being where the action was—especially action that was part of something bigger than herself. She could credit that desire with growing up in a country rife with violence—where sirens, bomb shelters, and the whisper of Apache helicopters were part of daily life.

At eight-years-old, Ma'ayan had moved with her father and younger sister to the United States. In comparison to Israel, life in the States was calm. She found herself seeking out the action everywhere—from grocery stores to her school classrooms.

In high school, she pioneered an investigative journalism team for the school newspaper, often breaking stories that most observers would have thought beyond the capabilities of students. In a particularly damaging exposé, Ma'ayan's relentlessness uncovered a web of corruption involving the head of the bus system, who had embezzled tens of thousands of dollars from the district by using substandard parts for the bus fleet, resulting in a significant rise in accidents and injuries. Her published exposé resulted in national publicity, a high-profile trial, and the revision of school district policies statewide.

Ma'ayan had experienced the excitement of discovery, and she was hooked. What began as the childhood thrill of finding dusty treasures in her *safta's* attic had turned into the thrill of finding out people's motives and actions.

Well before her high school graduation, the universities with prominent journalism programs had come knocking, and she had had her pick of the best. But no one expected that less than a year after choosing Columbia University, Ma'ayan would suddenly drop out. At the time, she cited reasons ranging from boredom to a restrictive academic system. But she'd simply known she wasn't supposed to be there.

Her dropout baffled her friends, who felt she was throwing away an incredible opportunity. Her father was especially devastated. A widower, he had moved the family to the United States to give them every opportunity, and here was Ma'ayan, walking away from what he told her would be her only weapon of success in a competitive world: a degree. But Ma'ayan knew her own internal desire for success far outweighed a slip of paper saying she had spent four years of her life somewhere. In fact, after dropping out, she felt doubly driven to prove herself without a university diploma.

Ma'ayan's sudden departure from her academic pursuits wasn't the last time she defied everyone's expectations. For better or worse, the hard-nosed journalist tended to make very snap decisions without always thinking them through. Marrying Nathan had been one (for worse). Moving to Fort Worth to raise her son had been another (for better).

Introspection ended as Ma'ayan arrived at the address OTF agent Peter Ashling had sent her. Nothing like a crime scene to keep her in the present.

Ma'ayan locked her helmet to a handle bar and walked to the circle that had formed around the body of a young woman.

"Hey guys," Ma'ayan said to the group of local law enforcement and OTF. She knew most of them.

"Hey Ma'ayan," Peter said, barely smiling. Something was heavier than usual.

Ma'ayan pulled out her notebook and looked closer at the victim. Though the woman's face was covered in blood, Ma'ayan had a terrible feeling.

Ma'ayan clenched her notebook, "Nikki!"

Tito Marnina shoved his hands deeper in his pockets and locked his jaw before answering, "Yes. Sorry we didn't warn you. We've all been a bit..." he coughed, "preoccupied."

Like the agents around her, Ma'ayan had seen it all. But this was the first time she'd known the victim.

Ma'ayan bent down and gently touched the hand of the woman she had known, if only as an acquaintance. "How long has she been here?"

Tito answered, "We got our dispatch less than an hour ago. An anonymous caller said he heard gunfire out here."

"Out here" was a vast field with a fence that ran as far as the eye could see.

Ma'ayan made a note. "Suspicious call?"

Peter nodded. "Someone wanted us to find her. Give us a few hours before you print anything. What you write could hurt us or help us."

A man stepped forward. Ma'ayan hadn't noticed him before. He had an official air like the rest but also something different. Mossad agent? She straightened and stood. His presence charged the scene with a controlled intensity.

The man spoke. "Yesterday in Tel Aviv, a university was bombed. One of your agents was present at the investigation."

Tito and Peter exchanged a look, then Peter asked, "And you think it was linked to Nikki's death?"

The Mossad agent looked at the two men, who wore white stones around their necks. "We think it's linked to all of you.

Chapter Two

THE FORENSICS TEAM finished, Nikki's body was taken away, and questions remained unanswered.

Ma'ayan perched on her bike, holding her notebook. She had over eighty of these—unlined and small enough to fit in her purse. She was never without her current notebook—ideas could arrive any time. Some pages were filled with mind maps, some with sketches of concepts that looked like a flower opening in time release, some with straight lists and other lists interrupted by stream-of-conscious "aha" moments that ran for pages.

Ma'ayan was just getting an idea when her stomach growled. The idea disappeared and she sighed. Time to drive to Sally's Diner.

Once there, she sat in her regular corner booth. Sally brought Ma'ayan a thick mug of black coffee without being asked, gave her a squeeze on the shoulder, and continued to serve other customers without saying a word.

Ma'ayan loved to come here. She could be alone in the noise instead of in the silence. Somehow, the distractions helped her focus, and Sally's wordless acknowledgment was a blessing. Ma'ayan hated chatting with waitresses. Nathan had never paid as much attention to her as he had to waitresses. He would practically invite them to join their table, asking question after question—things he never asked Ma'ayan. He had always seemed more interested in discovering who a stranger was than who his own wife was. All she had wanted was to be known by him.

Ma'ayan shook her head, sipped her coffee, and pulled

her notebook from her bag. It was filled with recent discoveries about this odd new task force who called themselves the Overcomers. She flipped back a few pages to her research:

The OTF Division deploys Overcomers for six-month assignments to the Middle East to work in fusion cells. The cells are made up of OTF, ISA, FBI, CIA, MI-5, and MI-6 agents who work directly with the office of intelligence on counterterrorism issues.

Aside from their official status, they're a bit strange. They sometimes know an attack is going to happen before it does. Unlike the psychics used by investigators, the Overcomers (only when asked) say they "hear from God."

They believe in prayer and practice a form of it called "intercession." This seems to involve interceding—praying—not from a focus on the bad circumstance but from a focus on its best outcome, a "greater reality."

To achieve a high level of proficiency, all those in the OTF require the highest level of realistic training, an "anytime-anyplace" concept. They are instructed in interactive animation, asynchronous and synchronous conferencing, student-to-student interface, student-to-instructor interface, laboratories, and practical exercises.

OTF units have access to the latest in high fidelity, virtual reality mission rehearsal systems. They must be able to interact with profiles in real world databases not ordinarily found in common simulation. They must be able to accurately navigate their whereabouts, at all times and in all conditions, while evading enemy forces, avoiding hazards at high speeds, and with perfect timing.

Part of their training systems includes language translation enhancements. Due to forward deployment, the OTF needs to communicate clearly and concisely with citizens from around the world.

Ma'ayan closed her notebook. She had heard a crazy rumor that some OTF agents, when they found themselves without their simultaneous translation technology, had suddenly been able to speak languages they had never encountered. She called it freaky. They called it divine impartation. Whatever it was, this task force was more a Force with a capital F.

They were going to make a great news feature. She hoped they could all stay alive to see it.

Ma'ayan's phone rang just as Sally brought her usual: bacon, eggs, and Texas Toast. Ma'ayan never had been one for food trends, and she was glad Sally's Diner had ignored them too.

She recognized the number and picked up.

"Hi, Peter."

A plate crashed in the diner kitchen.

"Sounds lively wherever you are."

"As lively as bacon and eggs can get." She took a bite of her toast.

"You didn't invite me to breakfast?"

She laughed. "Invite yourself next time."

"Actually, I am calling with an invitation.

Ma'ayan could feel some part of her stomach dancing with the toast. "Intriguing. Go on."

"You're researching us. I thought you might like to come to one of our meetings."

Ma'ayan's reporter instincts surged. "When and where?"

•ך•

The sun was low in the sky when Ma'ayan pulled up in front of a red house at the end of a long, gravel drive lined with cars.

The spring day had been warmer than she'd dressed

for, and she was hot and tired. After a few mediocre inter-
views and a failed attempt to contact the Mossad agent
she'd met that morning, Ma'ayan hoped that this evening
would redeem a rough day.

She stood her bike, pulled off her helmet, and ran her
fingers through her flattened hair. Did she look as tired as
she felt?

She walked the stone path through a garden wild with
colorful flowers. She recognized only a few: lantana, zin-
nias, and an expanse of purple hydrangeas. The only part
of the house not blazing with color was the white door.
Ma'ayan stepped onto the porch and knocked, surprised
that she felt faintly nervous. Did these people do any
weird rituals? Worse, would she have to endure a kind of
religious service?

A large, smiling woman opened the door. Her dark forehead was faintly gleaming with sweat beneath her yellow
turban.

"Ma'ayan. I'm glad you'll be joining us this evening. I'm
Della. Welcome to my home."

Della hugged Ma'ayan before she could protest. It was a
massive, motherly hug that seemed to push away all of the
day's stress. When Della released her, Ma'ayan felt something odd and unfamiliar—peace. It surprised her not just
because she never felt peace, but because this woman had
known Nikki and, despite that loss, was extending joy and
warmth.

"Come in." With a sweeping gesture of her arm, Della
invited Ma'ayan through an art-lined entryway into a spacious but packed living room. Tito and Peter. Morgan the
Creole, shaved-headed sniper. The tiny but fiery young
Yola. And Jesse Mae True, a woman of Della's indetermi-
nate age but with the opposite physique—she could be an

ex-marathon runner. Ma'ayan had met all but one of the people in the room, a man talking with Jesse Mae.

Peter saw Ma'ayan and walked over to her, giving her hand a squeeze. When he released it, she could feel the pressure throughout her body. It took her a second to hear him saying, "Welcome. You know everyone?"

Before she could respond, the unknown man approached them.

"We haven't met. I am Ishay." He spoke with the Hebrew accent Ma'ayan had lost.

"Shalom," she responded.

He smiled. "Barukh ha-ba. Welcome."

Della entered the room, a book held high. "If you don't have sweet tea, get yourself some and sit yourself down. We're beginnin'."

Ma'ayan's previous anxiety returned. Della was holding a big black Bible, Old and New Testaments—the Christian version. She sighed. Her gut instincts at the door had been right. Well, the religious fanaticism would add to the story.

She pulled out her notebook and glanced around as everyone found a place to sit. Peter was sitting cross-legged in front of the fireplace. Above the mantel hung a large plague: "As He is, so are we in this world. —1 John 4:17"

Ma'ayan wondered if they were into Jews for Jesus. What did they call themselves, Messianic Jews? She tried to turn off her cynicism. Report, don't judge.

Della held out the Bible, closed her eyes, and began to pray. Ma'ayan started taking transcripts.

"Abba, Abba, Abba. We thank you for Nikki's life. We thank you for the honor of knowing her and working with her. We bless her family with peace. We bless Tito with peace. We bless him today with an increased awareness of the hand of God on his life. We bless him with the para-doxical peace only a warrior knows in every circumstance.

We bless him with heaven's extraordinary bounty and promise—here on earth."

Ma'ayan lifted her eyes to look at Tito, whose head was in his hands. She realized that he and Nikki had been an item. Poor guy.

Della rested her massive hand on Tito's shoulder. In seconds, the entire room had surrounded him. Through a gap between Peter and Yolanda, Ma'ayan could see Tito lift his hands from his face.

Tito started speaking. "And to those who took Nikki, I say 'be found.' Be found by the Father of forgiveness. Be found by the mercy and love that end violence."

Ma'ayan stopped writing. She could hardly believe her ears. The rumors were true: This Overcomer was praying for Nikki's murderers. Was Tito crazy?

Jesse Mae began to speak. "We bless Nikki's family with peace. We bless Tito with peace."

They're all crazy, thought Ma'ayan. But she found herself caught up in these prayers, blessings, whatever they were. She watched the tight circle of people who called themselves Overcomers, and she wondered if maybe they lived up to their name.

Yola stepped back from the circle and bent over, supporting herself with her hands on her knees. The young girl began to speak from some place deep within her.

"All of creation waits. All of creation waits for you to walk in your destiny. When you do, you defeat death. Your destiny was shaped in heaven, and death has no hold on heaven. Bring heaven to earth. Bring light to dark. You have me within you. With me, you overcome all."

Ma'ayan started imagining titles for news features: Zany Prophets of the Lone Star State. Necklace-Wearing Task Force to Save the World. But even as her mind was flying with skepticism, her heart sensed it was all somehow genuine.

TEL AVIV, ISRAEL

Shafiq Karim waited until the professor's body was taken away. The ISA agent came over to him and put his hand on the Overcomer's shoulder. "I'm afraid you all are a target."

"Yes."

"That's all you're gonna say about it?"

Shafiq turned to the man. "I'd rather do than say."

The man smiled. "Of course. I forget who I'm talking to. Look. I know what you all can do. I've seen the crazy stuff no one would believe. I've seen you practically put people back together again. What is it, 'heal the sick,' right?"

"Right."

"Well, he was an old man. If it's any consolation, he would have gone soon. Maybe it was his time."

Shafiq had heard this before. He had thought it before. But he made no allowance for death by hate. Dr. Uziel had deserved to die in his sleep, not to be blown to bits by a terrorist bomb.

He sighed. He'd done everything he could do. The professor was dead. He could only hope he was able to save the next one.

Chapter Three

AFTER HER PRAYER, Yola sank to a sitting position on the floor, gently swaying.

Morgan, standing still and looking normal, quietly added, "Give us strength."

His arm, bare and black to the sleeve of his t-shirt, bulged with muscles Ma'ayan hadn't known existed. How interesting that the strongest-looking one on the team is asking for strength, she thought.

Ishay's head was tilted upward, his eyes open to the bare ceiling.

Peter's head was bowed, eyes closed tight and a hand to his heart.

Della was nodding rhythmically. She clapped her hands and said loudly, "Let's get His super on our natural!"

With that, the circle broke, and everyone returned to their places.

Peter lifted an eyebrow at her. She faintly shrugged her shoulders. What to think? What to say?

Della, who seemed to be the emcee, looked around the room. "Remember, we are children of God, filled with the same Holy Spirit as Jesus was, with the same opportunity to live as He lived on Earth. In fact, that's His plan. In John 17:18, He said to the Father, 'Just as You sent Me into the world, I also have sent them into the world.'"

"We are the 'them' He's talkin' about. We are the sent ones."

She walked over to the mantel and pulled down a ceramic bowl. From it, she picked out a penny and held it up. "Any time you find a penny, you don't need to think about luck. Read it and remember: "In God we trust" and "one cent—one sent. You are sent."

Della began carrying the bowl around the room, and each person chose a penny in silence. Ma'ayan held hers, and that sense of hollowness from this morning returned. Even though she'd forgotten lunch, she knew the feeling had nothing to do with her empty stomach.

Della placed the bowl back on the mantel and added, "That penny is a reminder; when you trust in God, when He sends you out, you have Him with you. This is a new season, so I thought it would be a good time for a new prayer. Here it is: I arise in darkness without fear, with Your super on my natural. Thank You for revealing secrets, solving mysteries, providing solutions. As You are, so am I. 'In God we trust.' I am one sent.

"As for sending out," she placed her hand on Ishay's shoulders, "I turn it over to this man, whose blood pumps through a heart that belongs to Israel. Tell us."

Ishay stood. "I am returning to Israel. You know of the bombing that occurred at the university. The professor was one of us. At first, our local agents thought he had been killed for discovering something. That may be. But as the Mossad agent said this morning, it is possible that we, the Overcomers, are the targets."

He paused to look around the room. "Our enemy is not just Hamas or Al-Qaeda. It is not whoever killed Nikki. Our enemy is evil. The absence of love. That evil is everywhere, but so is love. So are we.

"That said, we do face a new threat. Though we aren't sure yet what it is, we need to be ready for it. Jesse Mae had another dream."

Ma'ayan tried to keep her face blank. A dream? These people were galvanizing forces based on a dream?

Della, who seemed slightly telepathic, added, "We all know the power of Jesse Mae's dreams. They've been confirmed one-hundred percent." She crossed to Jesse Mae and squeezed her shoulder.

Jesse Mae began, "A little girl, eight or nine-years-old, was walking in a field of landmines. She had vision to see where they were, even though they were well hidden. The mines had been placed to kill her friends, and she knew she had the power to help them. She was carrying a green pen with a daisy at the end. At each land mine, she stopped and touched the pen to the sensors. They turned to daisies."

Ma'ayan couldn't keep her face blank this time. When she had left Israel for the United States with her family, her *safta* had given her a pen to write with on the flight. It was green. With a daisy at the end. She still kept it on her desk.

Jesse Mae was smiling at her. "It's your pen, isn't it?"

Her voice almost a whisper, Ma'ayan spoke. "How did you know this?"

Jesse Mae said, "Like you, I have friends in high places. I just practice listening."

Ma'ayan's head was swirling.

Della started speaking, "We listen here," she pointed down, "and here," she pointed up. "Down here, all kinds of good and bad things are happenin'. But we usually only hear the bad things, especially on the news. Violence. Murder. Mayhem. Up here—and I do mean 'here,' not 'there'—good things are waiting for us to pull them down into the mess we make on this earth.

"Ma'ayan, we need the world to know that there is more than fear. As things appear to get worse, we need to remind ourselves to hope for things to get better."

An oracle. That's what Della reminded Ma'ayan of: an oracle. The riddle-like wisdom wasn't making sense at the moment, but Ma'ayan scribbled notes to mull over later.

Odd as she was, Della exuded a peace that permeated her home. Ma'ayan wrote: It's like a safe house. Washes away the dust of the everyday with something better than water.

In the silence that followed Della's exhortation, Ishay clarified, "As you know, most of the mainstream news seen on home televisions and computers these days is managed, even manipulated, for the purposes of the agency releasing that news. And usually that purpose isn't pure. We need someone to write for both Middle East and U.S. syndication. Someone who understands both cultures."

"Other agents have also had dreams of warning. We want to be preemptive. We aren't vain enough to think we are the only target. We might be the gateway to something bigger because we represent the things our enemies will be most afraid of. Things that will prevent their larger plans."

Ishay was looking at Ma'ayan. "You are a trusted figure in the media. I think you are here to write about the Overcomers—to give people hope that they can be Overcomers, too. And I think you must come to Israel to do it."

He paused and looked at her with something more than his eyes. "Will you?"

Ma'ayan, her notebook long forgotten, just blinked. A thousand thoughts surged through her simultaneously: Ishay spoke with the same authority Yola did, though with the composure of a seasoned speaker. A power was filling the room that made the unshaven hair on her legs stand on end. Daisy pens, daisy pens—telepathy? She and Eitan had already been planning a summer trip to Israel for his graduation. She had forgotten dinner with him tonight. These people were beginning to scare her. She needed to pee. She had forgotten dinner with Eitan—again! Israel. Israel.

Without thinking, but with her mind fully engaged, she heard herself saying, "Yes."

Chapter Four

Ariel, Israel

L IVING IN A desert, Nasser never thought it could feel so good to be out of the rain. These days, he enjoyed few luxuries. One was a bottle of ha'arak. And tonight, the other was a roof over his head. Well, a partial roof. This part of the lab had more or less withstood the blast.

All of this bombing and killing. He had often wondered why his fellow countrymen fought so fervently over a few barren hills. And the Israelis—why all the fuss about this piece of arid sod known as the Holy Land? Sometimes Nasser thought humans had no sense at all. He coughed violently, shifted his weight, and took a swig from the bottle. He was the last one to criticize.

Homeless, jobless, drunk—those were the only skills on his curriculum vita now. Just three years ago, he'd been a prominent chemist in this very industrial park in Ariel, Israel. A small, young city still trying to be recognized as one, Ariel was the flagship of a daring new approach to peace in the Middle East.

Ariel's visionary mayor Yaniv Lieberman had revolutionized the way the world thought about peace. "Peace Through Economic Initiative" was more than a slogan; it had become a reality. Mr. Lieberman had personally directed the creation of an industrial park formed of a combined Palestinian and Israeli workforce of 5,000 employees. These two, warring, half-brother nations working in factories side by side? Impossible! Yet, the idea had worked.

The mayor believed people would grow to respect their coworkers. What happens when you work with someone day after week after month after year? When you see pictures of their children and grandchildren, husbands and wives, and aunts and uncles? When you grieve over a cancer diagnosis or death? You begin to see your fellow worker not as an enemy across the perimeter barricade but as the man or woman across from you on the assembly line or lab table: a person with feelings, hopes, dreams, desires, and needs just like yourself. Nasser had watched it happen. He had been a part of it.

Little by little, this newborn community grew into a vocational redeemer. It restored the common bonds of humanity that had been violently snatched away by "holy" wars.

Investors from all over the world saw the economic opportunities and began to pour in. In a matter of years, Ariel was producing annual revenues of five billion dollars generated from over one hundred and fifty separate businesses. And all of those business factories employed both Israelis and Palestinians. Nasser had loved working in this place.

He took another swig. The smell of alcohol triggered memories of his lab with all its chemicals. He had been good. He whispered to the ha'arak, "I have a Ph.D. from the Lebanese University. He coughed again and then nodded to confirm this, adding, "Even better: I had Israeli friends. Can you believe it?"

He smiled, whispering again, "Can you believe it?"

But by the time he finished asking the question for the second time, Nasser was thinking of another circumstance. His smile fell away in the dark.

He had brought his wife of fifteen years and his two gorgeous daughters to show them the lab where he worked. With pride, he had given them a tour, saying, "When you think of me during the day while I'm at work, you will be able to picture where I am." He had brought them to lunch at the cafeteria and sat them down with plates of musaka'a while he ran back to his office to get the za-atar spice his wife liked on her pita.

It was a terrorist bomb. The Palestinian Liberation Organization quickly claimed responsibility and even condemned their own brethren who worked in the lab for selling out to the enemy for money.

Alcohol became Nasser's only love after he lost all three of his. But the bottles never loved him back. They gave him greater emptiness after the initial burn of hope. They left him with less and less of himself.

The streets had become his home, except for the nights it rained. Then this condemned building became a bitter reminder of the ruined state of Nasser's own life. Occasionally, another filthy wanderer would curl up in a blackened corner, but mostly, Nasser's companions were rats.

Nasser was startled from his musings by footsteps. Though he cared little for his life, fear clenched his chest. Hoodlums would think nothing about eliminating a homeless drunk. In fact, they would probably enjoy it. This world was filled with such violence. Nasser's blood, thick with alcohol, began to pulse hard in his temple as his imagination leapt into action.

The footsteps were heading right to him. He squeezed his eyes shut, "Dear Allah!" he cried out silently, "save me!"

When Nasser dared to open one eye to see his executioners coming, he heard them begin to talk, and he could see the silhouette of their heads. How had they not noticed him? In a second of clarity, he realized they were on the other side of a shorter, broken wall just in front of him. He was laying in what had been a hallway, his back against the base of a more-or-less intact wall. Maybe if he didn't move they wouldn't see him.

Nasser began to focus on what the two men were saying as he clamped his hand over his mouth to keep from coughing.

One man spoke in hushed English with a heavy Russian accent. "I suppose you know the risk I take in coming here. Are you serious about this?"

An Arab accent answered, "General, seriousness is not the question. The question is whether a creation of this magnitude is possible."

"I think the question is: Can you provide the money? And I think you cannot. I must leave. I refuse to waste my time with dreamers." The General turned and started to go.

The Arab reached for his shoulder. "General Nikolayev, we already have the money. Before Azzam gives it to you, he wanted your personal guarantee that it will be effective."

The heads moved together as the Russian General yanked the Arab nose to nose. "Tell Azzam the virus has reached its final stages. It is ready. Once released, it will reach as far and wide as we promised. I do not like to be doubted. This meeting is a waste of my time."

The General said the last words in a careful staccato before pushing Azzam's messenger back in disgust. The Arab man mumbled a prayer in Arabic.

The General stalked off, passing close to Nasser and muttering under his breath in Russian. Nasser only caught the English words "Dead Sea."

Nasser was squeezing the bottle with one hand and his mouth with the other. The conversation had sobered him better than a carafe of Turkish coffee. He heard only a few more hushed and unintelligible tones before the pair quickly left. He slowly lowered his hand from his mouth, remembering to breathe. His mind began to race along with his heart.

The conversation Nasser had overheard would mean more deaths. More wives and daughters lost. But the fear he had felt when he first heard footsteps was transforming into a strange and forgotten feeling: hope. Allah had put him in a place where he could make a difference. He could help people. Many people. But how? He set the ha'arak down, careful not to make a noise in case the men were still nearby.

He heard another sound and sucked in his breath. He exhaled as the silhouette of a rat appeared on the half wall where he had seen the men's heads moments before. Nasser's dim eyes began to focus. Yes, he could help stop the infestation of hate.

He looked down at the abandoned bottle. "You know, it's been a long time since I sold any information to my friend, Shafiq."

Chapter Five
Fort Worth, Texas

M A'AYAN BURST INTO the kitchen. Eitan was at one end of the kitchen table, leaning over his laptop. The other end of the table was set for dinner. Which she had forgotten.

Eitan looked up at her with a blank face.

She held out her arms. "I am so, so sorry. That group I told you about invited me to one of their meetings. Way out in the middle of nowhere."

She came over to Eitan, putting her arms around his shoulders, continuing, "There was no cell reception, and I didn't want to stop when I got to town. I'll make it up to you. Dinner at the Capital Grille. Appetizers, dessert, you can sip my wine...."

"Mom, chill. I know you." Eitan reached up and hugged his mom's arms. "Since I was a kid, you've kept mayo that's been expired for at least five years. I learned to cook to keep from being poisoned by the contents of the fridge."

She laughed and gave his shoulders a squeeze. "Guilty as charged."

He squeezed her back. "Tonight, I made cholent. It gets better the longer it sits."

"You made cholent?" Ma'ayan walked over to the stovetop and lifted the lid off a pot of aromatic beef stew.

"It smells divine. What did I do to deserve you? Seriously, I do this too often. Dinner at the Grille as an apology."

Eitan closed his laptop, stood, and stretched. "Mom,

we're saving for Israel, remember? I'd rather have schwarma with chips and pita in Tel Aviv than a four-course meal in Fort Worth."

Israel.

"Um, yeah. We have a lot to talk about. You sit, I'll serve. I have to do something with my Jewish guilt."

Eitan laughed. "Glad I didn't inherit that."

"Yeah, you're lucky. Wait till you meet your great-grand-mother. Safta Bracha makes me look like a lamb."

Ma'ayan ladled the steaming stew into the bowls Eitan had set out.

He walked to the counter. "There's more."

He lifted a tea towel off the cutting board and revealed a loaf of challah so golden and perfect that Ma'ayan wanted to cry. "What, you're adding insult to injury? Why do you want to go to Columbia University? You could open a restaurant."

Eitan smiled and set the challah in the center of the table. "I don't think I can change the world with a restaurant. These are all skills to get girls. Sorry, Mom, I'm just practicing on you." He tousled her hair.

How did he grow up so fast? How was she having adult conversations with the little boy who had run around in footed pajamas as a toddler? How had he learned to make bread? She loosened the stopper from the Shiraz she'd opened yesterday and poured herself a generous glass.

"You're right. I can see you sitting in the U.N. building in a well-cut suit, giving a speech that will ignite world peace. You have the ability to communicate with people three times your age. Do you remember when you were nine? You calmed down a woman in the grocery store who had lost her wallet. I think you even reminded her to breathe."

He smiled and poured himself a glass of mineral water. He was the only American teenager she knew who liked mineral water.

He raised his glass. "To peace."

"And to life. L'chaim."

The stew was delicious. One of the few good things Nathan had left his son was a love for good food and the passion to cook it. If only her ex-husband had been able to love people as much as perfectly-flipped omelets and fluffy blintzes.

Eitan broke off a rounded lump of challah. "So, what did we need to talk about?"

Oh. Right. "Well, about Israel. The timing might be a bit awkward."

Eitan fixed his mother with that rare gaze of steely inflexibility. "You're not cancelling."

"No, no, no, no, no." She held her hands up. "Don't worry. It's just that I've been invited to go sooner than this summer."

"Go on."

"The OTF might be a terrorist target..." She paused.

Eitan set down his bread, "Gee, Mom, that's a great way to start convincing me this is a good idea."

"Hey, you know very well I get in the middle of anything and everything. Blood, guts, and all. I've made it this far."

"Maybe you're pressing your luck."

"We don't believe in luck, remember?"

Eitan lifted an eyebrow. "Unfortunately true when it comes to tests. Study beats luck every time."

"Speaking of which, how did the math test go?"

"I did well, I think."

"You always do. I'm very proud of you."

"Meanwhile, in Israel..."

"How did you get so smart, anyway?"

He reached across the table and tapped her on the forehead. "You passed on some of those brains. Israel."

"Right. I met another member of the OTF tonight. His name is Ishay. He's based in Israel and is returning there… this week." She looked at her son and bit her lip. "He wants me to go, too. He gave me a few reasons, but even though I don't see the logic in them, my gut tells me there's something to be discovered."

Ma'ayan absently took a bite of stew and added, "Ishay is from Israel. So was the Mossad agent, of course. Safta Bracha used to tell me, 'Coincidence is God winking at you.'"

They ate in silence for a few moments before Ma'ayan continued, "I don't get these people. Why do they meet in an old lady's house way out in farmland? What does she have to do with highly trained agents? Why are highly trained agents blessing people who murder and destroy? Do they really believe they can mitigate violence before it even happens? Who leads this group? Are the OTF like some government-sanctioned illuminati, hidden throughout society, readying themselves for some apocalyptic event?"

Eitan was looking at his mother with a bemused smile. "You have that look. The obsessive one that means you won't stop until you've answered all your questions."

Ma'ayan shrugged and drank her wine. "I'm a terrible mom. I should have been like your Aunt Amit. She always remembers dinner. She even cooks dinner."

"Stop fishing for complements. The wine is talking." He took the last bite of his soup. "This might be a great opportunity for you. You always tell me to take every opportunity. Maybe you should go to Israel early."

"The assignment might last months. I'm not missing my only son's graduation."

"Sleep on it."

Sleep. Oh, sleep. Ma'ayan yawned. "Leave the dishes. I'll get them in the morning. Thanks for a delightful dinner."

"You're welcome." Eitan flipped open his laptop. Ma'ayan glanced at his screen. Multiple windows were open, some with codes and colors that looked like coordinates to foreign worlds.

Ma'ayan shook her head. "Whatever you're doing with all that nonsense, be sure to rest your eyes regularly."

"Yes, ma'am," he said with an exaggerated, Texan drawl. It was his nickname for her—a play on her name—that he used when he was done receiving advice.

She kissed Eitan on the cheek, picked up her bag, and headed for her room. She decided to skip typing up her notes and pulled on a nightshirt instead. Curling up under the covers, she checked her phone, glad she'd remembered to silence it during dinner.

Two new voicemails.

One from her sister, Amit. Ma'ayan could almost see the exclamation marks in her message: "Hello, Ma'ayan!! I was just thinking of you and Eitan. I am menu planning for Passover next week and just wanted to confirm that you both are coming!?! We'd love to have you!!! Dad's excited. Do let me know. Bye, honey!"

And one from Peter: "So I won't present this as anything other than a social SOS. Friends of the family invited my parents and me to a dinner. I'm supposed to bring someone. The hosts are probably old school—need a balanced table or something like that. Save me? Tomorrow night at seven, but cocktails at six. Semi-swanky attire, judging by the large columns on the front of their house. I can pick you up at quarter to six. Say yes."

Ma'ayan's face was covered with a smile when she

finished listening. Never mind that Peter was younger than her. He was funny. He got her.

She was already thinking about what to wear. But she'd promised herself to not date men until Eitan graduated.

Now she had two things to sleep on.

Chapter Six

PETER WAS RIGHT on time. Eitan stood at the side of the window, peeking around the edge of the curtain to keep from being seen.

"He's younger than you are."

"Gee thanks. This from the son who is convincing me to go out with him in the first place."

Ma'ayan was checking her mascara in the hall mirror. She rarely wore the stuff, and now her top and bottom lashes were sticking together. She kept them apart long enough to look down at her blue silk shirt and the black pants. She didn't own a dress, hadn't since she'd become "one of the guys" after her husband left her.

She asked her son, "You're sure this outfit looks OK?"

Eitan stepped back from the window and looked his mother up and down. "Mom, you look amazing. Besides, even if you didn't, you don't have any time to change."

The doorbell rang in confirmation.

"I'll get it." Eitan opened the door and stood in front of Peter, looking him up and down the way he had just done with Ma'ayan.

Peter returned the size-up, smiled, and held out a white rose corsage curled in a deep green leaf. "I don't think this will work with your t-shirt."

Eitan smiled and extended his hand, "I'm Eitan. Ma'ayan's son."

Peter shook his hand firmly. "Quite a pleasure. According to your mom, I'm talking with the most perfect son in the world."

Eitan laughed, shook his head, and stepped back into the house, "Come in. Mom's ready."

Ma'ayan felt like she was in high school again. Eitan, who actually was in high school, looked more composed than she did.

Peter held the corsage toward her. "Flashback to prom?"

She laughed, and he stepped closer so he could pin the rose to her shirt. "If this was prom, I'd be wearing so much taffeta you couldn't get close enough to pin anything on me."

This time, Peter laughed. Eitan was silent, watching them both. Ma'ayan felt her face starting to flush. "Well, we don't want to be late for gin and tonics."

She turned to Eitan, giving him a hug. "Honey, take a break tonight. You've been studying too hard. Watch a movie or something. Have fun."

Before releasing the hug, he said, "I will if you will." Then, as he kissed her cheek, he whispered, "Don't use me as an excuse to avoid love."

With her son's words swirling in her head, Ma'ayan began her first date in almost twenty years.

•וׁ•

It was a pleasant break to ride in a car. No helmet. No worrying about her center of gravity. The flat, Texan landscape flew by, and Ma'ayan sat back in the leather seat and began to relax. "So our hosts are...who?"

"Victor and Karla Wexler. Old money. Messianic Jews who support Israel."

Peter turned to look at her before returning his eyes to the road. "Confession: you're not just invited to balance out the table. In fact, Ishay is coming, so we'll be an odd number anyway." In an exaggerated English accent, he continued, "The butler will be horrified."

"So why am I invited?"

"You're quite the journalist, asking the 'who, what, when, where, why, and how.' You've got a few to go."

"How about this: What am I tonight? A guest of the Wexler's or the date of Peter Ashling?"

He smiled at her, showing his white teeth. "Both. But I'm happiest with the second."

Ma'ayan was silent for a moment. "That works for me. My confession? I haven't been on a date since Eitan's father was courting me. Well, courting is a large word." She bit her lip, reminding herself not to dwell.

Peter looked at her with his eyebrows arching, "Seriously?"

"I guess you're not supposed to admit that on a first date." Ma'ayan laughed and sighed, "Hey, the stakes change when kids are involved. I didn't want to expose Eitan to men who probably wouldn't want to play father. Plus, I got a bit consumed with my job for, oh, a dozen years, until I broke away from television."

"Well, I'm honored you're breaking your pattern for me."

She didn't have time to respond. The car slowed and Peter said, "Here we are."

He pulled up to a gate that glided open at their arrival. The car started down a long, treeless drive toward an enormous house. There were indeed pillars. Eight of them. The mansion could be the set for a twenty-first century remake of *Giant*.

Peter parked the car near two others. Ma'ayan laughed. "What, no valet parking? Really."

Ma'ayan had been to homes of extreme wealth before. She'd never been overly impressed. It just seemed like a lot of fuss and overhead.

She and Peter ascended—that was the only word for it—the very white stairs to the door. A doorman opened it before they knocked and escorted them into a parlor.

Inside, five people stood around a mini bar: one couple in their sixties, one in their seventies, and Ishay Koen.

The blond, trim, sixty-something woman came over to hug Peter. "Darling! So glad you could come, honey."

Peter gave her a hearty hug. "May I introduce Ma'ayan Bracha. The journalist I told you about. Ma'ayan, this is my mother, Elise."

"A pleasure."

The group moved forward and began introducing themselves. Elise's quiet and grim husband, Mike. Victor Wexler, tall and slim in an impeccably tailored suit and goatee. Karla Wexler in a dress that women of a certain age wear to flatter their necks and arms.

Ishay nodded at Peter and Ma'ayan, raising his designer-suited arm in welcome.

Ma'ayan was glad she'd chosen her silk shirt, but she wished she'd added a necklace or earrings.

Karla ended the introductions with a shake of her glass, "What would you like to drink?"

Ma'ayan pointed to Karla's glass, "Gin and tonic? I'll have the same."

Peter smiled and shook his head, "Just the tonic for me, thanks."

The party found perches on various pieces of furniture upholstered in elegant chintzes and brocades.

"So, Ma'ayan," began Karla from her wingback chair beneath a massive oil painting depicting a fox hunt. "I love your work. When you did television, I watched most every feature you did, didn't I, hon?" She smiled at her husband.

Victor smiled back at his wife. "Absolutely. Karla and I are avid news junkies. We don't tend to make much time for print these days, so I'm afraid we haven't been following you as closely."

Ma'ayan took a sip of the drink that Peter brought her. "I miss television now and then, but it's quite nice to be able to freelance for print."

Ishay leaned forward, "And you are researching the OTF. Is that a personal interest?"

Ma'ayan looked at Peter and hoped she didn't blush. "I didn't know the OTF existed until I ran into Peter at my son's soccer game a month or so ago."

Elise looked at Peter, "Oh, that's right. You took Jimmy to some of the games this season, didn't you?" Elise shifted her gaze to Ma'ayan. "Peter is a wonderful uncle. Loves children."

Ma'ayan was wishing she hadn't let Eitan convince her to come. On the Ashling's side, this didn't seem a date so much as a trial by parents, dipped in sugary, Southern sweetness. But as for the Wexler's and Ishay, she sensed multiple ulterior motives ricocheting across the room.

Changing the subject, as if reading her mind, Victor leaned back and crossed his legs. "Ma'ayan, you're a clever reporter. Why do you think you're here?"

Years of cutting to the chase taught Ma'ayan to state things like they were, regardless of how they landed. "Here goes," she told herself and answered: "I have a few theories. They vary from person to person. I think you and Karla want me to write something for you. I know that Ishay does. I think Peter's parents are wondering what he's doing with an older woman who probably doesn't want more children. And I'll tell Peter what I think later." She smiled at him, eyebrow raised, and took a sip of her drink in the awkward silence that followed.

The butler wisely chose that moment to announce, "Dinner is served."

Chapter Seven

Ariel, Israel

NASSER SAW HIM before he crossed the street. Shafiq was sitting at one of the outside tables, sunglasses on, back against the beam separating the café from the repair shop next door. He faced the direction Nasser was approaching. Nasser was glad to be on the man's good side. With his shaved head, thick neck, and air of power, Shafiq wasn't someone you'd want to cross.

Only two other tables were occupied. Nasser ran a hand through hair that hadn't seen soap in…how long? The thought of a coffee sounded like an exquisite luxury. And Shafiq would buy. In fact, he'd be paying Nasser well—enough to buy cases of ha'arak if he wanted.

Just before he reached the table, Nasser coughed violently, his lungs searing. This cold never seemed to leave.

"Peace be upon you," said Nasser, hitting his chest to keep from another cough.

"And upon you be peace. You are not well?" asked Shafiq.

Nasser shrugged and sat down, taking off his jacket. He waved a hand at nothing in particular. "The rain…"

The morning was warm and sticky after the rain, and Shafiq wore a shirt exposing his neck and part of his chest. Nasser tried not to stare at the white stone hanging there. The red lines in it made something in him uncomfortable.

Shafiq was already sipping a steaming glass of coffee. He ordered one for Nasser and lifted his jaw a bit. "So?"

Nasser cleared his throat and started coughing again.

The coffee arrived, and he took a drink, letting the hot liquid salve his throat. The cough subsided.

Shafiq watched him.

Nasser set down his glass and lowered his voice. "There are plans. Terrible plans to release a virus. I overheard a conversation between a Russian and an Arab. The Russian was General Nikolayev. And the Arab worked for a man named Azzam."

Shafiq set down his coffee and looked at the grounds now visible in the bottom of his cup. "What language were they speaking?"

"English."

"And the Arab—could you tell where he was from by his accent?"

"My English is not that nuanced."

"Did any associations come up while they spoke?"

"What do you mean?"

"Did either man remind you of other people you have known? Did any memories arise when you heard them or now as we speak about them?"

Nasser thought those questions odd. He hesitated. He didn't want to admit he'd been quite drunk when eavesdropping and so couldn't remember too many details. But he also felt like a thought might come to him if he waited for it. He took a long drink of his coffee and remembered the feel of the wall against his back as he'd lain in the cold darkness.

He did remember something: "The Arab man said a quick prayer when the Russian grabbed him—he doubted that the buyer had the money. The Arab man sounded like the Iranian grocer I used to visit in the market. The grocer had lived on the coast of the Persian Gulf, and he used to tell stories of his childhood when I bought pomegranates from him."

A group of young Haredi Jewish men walked by the cafe, their wide-rimmed black hats shadowing their faces. Shafiq looked in their direction, his eyes invisible behind the dark lenses.

Nasser started coughing again and couldn't stop. This time the coffee didn't help.

Shafiq shifted his gaze to Nasser. In the same tone of voice, he said, "I command this cough to cease. Peace to your lungs. Be healed."

Shafiq slapped his hand palm down on the table. The coffee glasses rattled on their saucers.

Nasser's breath caught in his throat. He felt at first like he was going to choke. But the sensation turned into a fiery warmth that ran down his throat to his lungs and back. A memory of his chemistry lab popped into his head: bubbling, fizzing solutions churning on Bunsen burners.

The image faded and Nasser's cough was gone. He took a cautious breath and felt good. In fact, he could actually feel his lungs. He looked across at Shafiq. "What was that?"

"My people, the ones who wear these…" he lifted up the white stone with those haunting red streaks, "we follow someone who taught we have God in us, just as He did. We walk in the power He gave us."

Nasser swallowed, still amazed at how soothed his throat was. "Who is this person?"

"Yeshua."

Nasser looked at Shafiq. He would never have thought such a man would believe the teacher Yeshua was more than just that—a teacher. Even the Jews didn't believe He was God.

Shafiq was looking at him. "You don't have to believe in Him for Yeshua to heal you. But it's not a bad idea."

Shafiq slid an envelope across the table to Nasser, whose throat and lungs were still tingling with warmth. "Don't buy ha'arak with this. It is time to start over. This is not payment. This is an investment. Don't disappoint me."

FORT WORTH, TEXAS

A painting of a large, white owl hung above Victor Wexler's seat at the head of the dining room table. The owl's eyes pierced through the dim room, bright like the candles.

Ma'ayan set down her heavy, silver spoon in the now-empty bowl in front of her. It had been filled with a transcendent celery root and apple soup.

As the butler removed her bowl, she looked at her host and Peter in turn. "Are you telling me the Overcomers are some sort of superhero pack? With powers?" She laughed, "I think you're looking for a comic book writer, not an investigative journalist."

Peter smiled. "Sorry to disappoint. None of us duck into phone booths and emerge in a red cape."

Ma'ayan cocked her head at him. "Of course not; no one uses phone booths anymore. For all I know, you dial a number on your smart phone, and the satellite zaps you with powers of flight."

The butler reappeared with a platter of smoked trout and a chutney of eggplant and green beans.

Victor started laughing. "My dear, you're confusing superhero with supernatural. We are talking about the latter, though it certainly creates the former. Those who want a rational explanation think of quantum physics and the fourth dimension. But I am speaking of a spiritual power that alters our natural world. Less mask-wearing action figures and more the symbolic owl."

He pointed behind him. "The owl sees in the dark. Its eyes are designed to collect and process any light in the darkness."

Ma'ayan looked up at the painting. Yes—even those painted eyes seemed to see through things.

Peter added, his own eyes flashing, "We are most effective in the dark. If we all show up in the light armed with flashlights and then turn them on—no effect. But when we show up in the dark with our flashlights—different story."

Victor nodded at Peter, "The Overcomers are trained to use spiritual abilities that most of us either never discover or let atrophy if we do."

Karla, looking at nothing in particular in the middle of the table, added, "I think of my children. I watched them learn to crawl, then walk, then run. They learned to make sounds, then words, then sentences. And now they study subjects in college that I didn't even know existed when I was their age."

She ran her fingers across an eyelet in the linen tablecloth and looked up at Ma'ayan. "You know how it is. Parents get to help their children develop skills they have the potential to use. But what if they have spiritual skills that remain undiscovered? I want my children to walk in their fullest abilities and destinies. I want every good thing for them."

Ma'ayan nodded. "Of course. Every parent does."

Peter's mother, Elise, who had been mostly quiet since the awkward drinks in the parlor nodded, "Yes."

Her husband reached over and squeezed her hand. Ma'ayan wondered if he ever spoke.

Ma'ayan visualized all of the people around her and their conversations as semi-transparent jigsaw puzzle pieces overlaying yesterday's murder, the bomb in Tel Aviv, and the circle of Overcomers praying in Della's living room.

She took a deep breath. "This all is the background to something. I got some of it last night at Della's. I'm guessing you need me to write about the OTF for reasons of publicity. Possibly to give them visibility that an as-yet-unidentified terrorist group assumes they'll avoid. Let me guess: Some terrorist plot is about to explode—probably literally. You want to scare the bad guys or give the OTF public support or both?

Victor meticulously cut a piece of his smoked trout, chewed, swallowed, and set down his fork and knife. He looked right at Ma'ayan and smiled. "Both."

"You're a reporter. You see far-reaching implications. Historically, every empire that stood against Israel was removed from power. The United States cannot remain passive about Israel. We already see the ramifications of our country's apathy toward her. Part of our longer-term strategy is to build awareness of Israel's significance. That's not necessarily part of this assignment, but it may help you see the broader scope we're addressing. One of your investigative gifts is carrying history into contemporary events, and you have a great track record doing it. So, yes, we do need your help."

A silence followed in which Ma'ayan sensed the courses of lives would be determined. She had the funny feeling hers was one of them, and she wasn't entirely sure she wanted to know how.

Ma'ayan took a deep breath. "Years ago, my news director asked me a question: 'Ma'ayan, what does a chiropractor do?' I answered, 'He manipulates in order to ensure you are properly aligned.' She nodded and told me I was no different. That I may need to manipulate things in my career as a journalist in order to properly align society. That it would all be for the greater good. At the time, I was young. I almost believed her. But who really has the right to make 'adjustments'?"

Ishay, who had been quiet for most of the meal, now

spoke. He looked around the table. "You have heard that natural gas has been discovered off-shore in Israeli waters. The Wexler's have been investing in the discovery of those gas reserves for over almost two decades. They have been working to help Israel create her own wealth. And it looks not just possible but probable. That is the good news. The bad news: an Overcomer in Israel had a vision that the terrorists are not just targeting OTF agents but also the off-shore gas plants. And Jesse Mae's dream of you, Ma'ayan... well, her dreams have served us more than well in the past. Unlike a traditional task force, the OTF values supernatural clues even more than natural ones. Visions, dreams— these are the realms of solutions we operate in."

Elise asked what Ma'ayan was already figuring out, "What connection is there between the OTF and the natural gas?"

Victor cleared his throat and looked at Karla; she gave a single nod.

He continued, "We're also primary financial backers for the OTF. In fact, we helped create them with our son, Jason—one of the alpha Overcomers. He is stationed in Israel and is a good friend of Ishay's. We think it likely that if the OTF is a target, so are any enterprises their backers fund."

Ishay added, "And we do need some healthy manipulation of the press." He winked and then grew sober. "Peter just confirmed that the OTF is a target. Ma'ayan, your guesses were all correct. The terrorists want to eliminate the OTF so they can carry out a bigger plan. A massive plan. And the terrorists themselves are likely an allegiance that has been building for years, gaining power because no one knows they exist—until now. They know the Overcomers could prevent whatever they are planning. Most Overcomers stay undercover, but the problem with walking in supernatural power is that people tend to notice." He gave a wry smile here. "So since the signs and wonders are growing, we decided to do what the enemy doesn't expect—to bring awareness to the Overcomers. To make the public aware of the 'superheroes' among them. To create a collective hope for powers of light that will diminish powers of darkness. To bring awareness to the Overcomer Task Force."

Despite the religious overtones of Ishay's speech, Ma'ayan felt the childhood thrill of attic treasures. "And I would be the first one to write about them."

Chapter Eight

Ariel, Israel

AZZAM WAS NOT happy, though only the men who knew him well could tell—not by any facial expression, but by a barely palpable shift in the atmosphere around him. A kind of airless pressure.

Jalil wasn't exactly happy, either. He hoped he wouldn't have to meet with any more generals in damp and dark places, but he couldn't afford to look as disapproving as Azzam and his henchmen. These people knew where Jalil's family lived.

The warehouse was hot. All the computers generated heat. Lots of heat. Jalil willed himself not to sweat more than he already was.

When angry, Azzam spoke slowly and with a frightening calm. With deliberate enunciation, he said, "He doubts me? He thinks I do not have the money? I have enough to buy him and his family's land ten times over and burn it."

Jalil ran his fingers under the edge of his kuffiya to wipe away the sweat on his forehead. He rubbed his hand on the white robes of his thawb. The reference to family wasn't lost on him. "Of course. I know this. I told him, sir. He was angry…"

Azzam and his assistants glowered at Jalil. Oh, how he wished Azzam had returned a day later. He could have dealt with this tomorrow after a good night's sleep. His neighbor's dog in the settlement had barked all night. Think.

"Sir, I serve you and your vision. I do what you ask of me without question. You are a powerful man, and I was honored to represent you to General Nikolayev even though he does not deserve the respect you do."

As he said the sugary words, Jalil's mouth tasted sour. He hoped his face did not show the disdain he felt.

Azzam's eyes narrowed just as the afternoon call to prayer brayed through the cement walls.

All of the computer techs went to their mats, facing Qiblah. Jalil joined the prayers, placing his thumbs to his earlobes and beginning, "Allahu Akbar. Allah is the greatest."

But just as he had said one thing to Azzam while thinking another, Jalil continued the salat recitation with the troubling feeling that he didn't believe what he was saying.

TEL AVIV, ISRAEL

Shafiq watched him approach from where he stood in the shade of a cypress tree in the Uziel garden. He barely recognized Jason Wexler. That was one of Jason's gifts: mutability. Today, he looked like an American tourist for a new, longer-term assignment: t-shirt and baseball cap, ripped jeans—as close to his real self as Shafiq had ever seen him. Jason could also look like a wealthy Scandinavian businessman with blonde hair and a penchant for saunas. Or he could wear a tzitzit and dark sidelocks and pass for an ultra-Orthodox Jewish scholar.

Like Leo Uziel had been.

Shafiq sighed, sad at the loss of his friend and informant, knowing he had lost much more than the sum of either part.

Jason opened the garden gate. They had agreed to meet openly, figuring that one or both of them would be followed anyway.

Jason nodded at Shafiq, extending his hand. The handshake pulled into a hug before the men stepped back, both of them at a momentary loss for what to say. They had agreed to meet in the wide open, right in front of the Uziel house.

Shafiq looked at the front door. "The family is inside."

"Such a tragedy."

Shafiq nodded. "Has anyone claimed responsibility for the bombing?"

Jason answered, "Unfortunately, yes. A new terrorist group. An alliance."

"A Russian-Islamic alliance, by any chance?"

Jason gave a half smile. "I shouldn't be surprised that you know."

He looked straight at Shafiq. "Doubly sad, this one. The Western world will have yet another opportunity to apply the generalization of fear and terror to all of your people. That, and this group calls itself Takbir."

Shafiq shook his head. He had heard the word takbir all his life. It was the inciting chant to which Islamic followers responded "Allahu Akbar, Allah is the greatest." In its best expression, takbir was a call to praise. In its worst, it was a call to jihad.

Jason adjusted his baseball cap and looked above a lemon tree into the bright, clear sky. "I wonder what they're planning"

"Possibly biological warfare."

"They have no idea what they're up against."

Shafiq gave a wry, half smile. "Neither did Pharaoh."

The men went inside to mourn with the mourners, hoping they had been overheard.

Fᴏʀᴛ Wᴏʀᴛʜ, Tᴇxᴀs

When Peter pulled his car up outside Ma'ayan's house, the porch light was on, but the living room lights were off. Ma'ayan knew Eitan was sitting in the dark with his laptop, waiting.

She worried Peter might try to walk her to the door and kiss her goodnight. Ma'ayan didn't think Eitan could handle that yet. She didn't think she could handle that yet.

Peter smiled in the darkness of the car, illuminated only by the lights on the dash. "Don't worry. I'll just wait for you to get in."

Ma'ayan gave a short laugh. "You're a smart one, you are."

"Well, I…"

And while Ma'ayan waited for him to finish his thought, Peter leaned over and gave her a quick kiss on the lips.

She was still wondering if it had really happened when he said, "There. You didn't have to second-guess anything. Go in before your son wonders if I'm making out with you. Sweet dreams."

"Yes." Ma'ayan fumbled for the door, stepped out, and said, "Thank you for an interesting evening."

"Hmm. I'll have to up my game, I guess. Interesting isn't the kind of original word I'd expect from a journalist."

She could see him wink in the light triggered by the opened passenger door.

Shaking her head, Ma'ayan smiled and walked to her house. "Good night, Peter."

She opened the front door, waved, and watched Peter's car pull out of the driveway.

Sure enough, Eitan was sitting on the couch, his laptop open and casting pale blue light on his face.

"So, Mom. Let's talk."

Ma'ayan sighed and sank onto the chair opposite her

son, wondering faintly if she really was the parent and Eitan the child, or if God had switched the parent-child order on her when she hadn't been looking.

He closed his laptop and smiled. "What was my favorite story as a kid?"

"Are we talking superheroes? Spiderman."

"Yes—no. The ancient ones."

"Samson. Sampson and Delilah. You always wanted his super powers."

Eitan shifted to stretch his legs out on the coffee table. "Yep. And even when he messed up—revealing the secret of his strength and then losing it—God used him anyway."

Ma'ayan narrowed her eyes at her son. "Are you hinting at something?"

"Of course. Remember how you've always told me I had special powers, just like Samson?"

Ma'ayan laughed. "And you complained that you couldn't pick up our house and move it to Israel. You wanted powers of physical strength, but I told you your powers were different. You have the power of unity, of peace. You bring it wherever you go."

Eitan shook his head. "That didn't go over so well with a five-year-old. But I am starting to see what you mean." He looked straight at his mother. "It looks like I can move our 'house' to Israel after all. I spoke to my teachers and the principal today."

Ma'ayan's mind snapped into focus. "What about?"

"I think you should go to Israel. For this assignment. Now. And I think I should come with you."

He didn't wait for her to respond, but continued, breaking his grownup manner with the little-boy excitement he occasionally forgot to mask. He pulled his feet from the coffee table and leaned toward her. "Here's the deal, Mom. I have A's in all my classes. I've already been accepted to Columbia on scholarship, and I'll be able to finish my independent study in journalism by shadowing a great journalist—you. I can keep up with work online and finish my classes long-distance. If you're still working when graduation nears, I can come back. Or not."

Ma'ayan felt like she was back on the playground with Eitan, only this time he was spinning the merry-go-round and she was riding it. She tried to think of a way to defer an answer until she could think more clearly. "Well, it's a thought. Maybe we can ask for a sign. A very concrete sign."

He smiled. "It came to the house right before you returned. Here."

Eitan handed her an unsealed envelope. Outside, it read: "To the Brachas, from the Wexlers."

Inside were two first class tickets to Tel Aviv. The departure date was in four days.

Eitan was watching her. "I almost forgot the other bit of interesting news the principal told me when he approved my trip; the school will be receiving a very large donation from the Wexler family for a new soccer field."

Chapter Nine

Ariel, Israel

NASSER STOOD AT the door hoping his clothes didn't smell too badly. He had done his best to look presentable, using the coffee shop's dingy bathroom to wash his face and hands.

He knocked at the door of the only man he thought might still—

The door opened, and Anastasii appeared. Nasser always forgot the left side of his former colleague's face had turned into a wound of burned flesh from the bombing. But when Anastasii smiled, a smile was all that showed. A smile filled Anastasii's face now as he stepped forward and embraced his friend.

"Nasser! Tell me you will stay this time. Nonna said she saw you on the street the other day. Come in, come in."

Anastasii didn't give Nasser time to protest but pulled him inside, calling for his wife in Russian. "Nonna! Nasser is here. Pour another cup of tea!"

Nasser really hoped he didn't smell. He remembered the pristine loveliness of Nonna's house. He'd come here with his own wife before…before.

Nasser tried to stay in the present. He felt relieved he wasn't shaking for ha'arak. In fact, he realized that not just his terrible, endless cold had disappeared after Shafiq's prayer but also his thirst for alcohol.

Nonna appeared from the kitchen, a quiet smile on her face. Less demonstrative than her husband, she looked at the man she'd only known as professional and well groomed. He now stood in her foyer resembling a life-long beggar. She looked past the deep stains of his jacket and the disintegrating hems of his pants. She looked past the scraggly beard into the man's eyes and saw what her husband had been trying to awaken during the years since the bombing: hope.

She gave a small nod, extending her hand. In her thick Russian accent, she said to Nasser, "We are so pleased you came. You will stay with us this time."

She turned to her husband and said in Russian, "He needs a vacation from his pain."

Nasser felt a warmth rise through him. He recognized something in her words, even though he did not understand them. He felt his spirit rise up. He started laughing. For the first time since he had lost his wife and children, he felt the hope of joy.

FORT WORTH, TEXAS

"Amit?"

"Ma'ayan! Hello dear! I—just a second," Amit's voice receded as she spoke to someone, "not there, darling. Put it in the trashcan. Yes. Good job. Ma'ayan? Sorry, Micah has started bringing in dead bugs. He was setting them on the breakfast dishes. So when are you arriving?"

"We can't make it."

A rare silence. Not even background noise from her reliably loud youngest nephew, the only one of her sister's children not yet in school.

Amit began to speak in her parent voice even though she was the younger sister, "Now, Ma'ayan, of course you can. Dad's expecting you. The kids are so looking forward to seeing Eitan. It's been since Hanukkah. You know we'd come to you if Hank could get off work. It's only a five hour drive."

Thank God for those five hours, thought Ma'ayan, meaning it like a prayer. To her, Galveston was city of broken dreams.

Always oppressed by thoughts of her previous life, Ma'ayan felt lighter when she said, "Eitan and I are flying to Israel."

She meant it. She hadn't fully committed until she said the words.

Amit was confused. "That's not till summer. What does that have to–"

"We're flying this week."

"For Passover? Why didn't you tell me? Does Dad know?" The little sister was finally emerging—whining and petulant.

Band-Aid, thought Ma'ayan. Rip it off fast. "Of course not, honey. It's work related. Just came up yesterday. I wasn't going to accept the assignment, but Eitan was also, um, invited. Tickets paid, the whole nine yards. He's actually the one who convinced me to go. I would never have missed his graduation. But he seems far more excited to walk the streets of the Holy Land than down an aisle to 'Pomp and Circumstance.' Go figure."

She was being facetious with the last sentence, but Amit, a celebrator of recognized achievements, took her seriously. "Oh, Ma'ayan. He can't possibly miss his high school graduation! He'll regret it for the rest of his life! Do you want me to talk to him? Maybe Hank? He's kind of a father figure for Eitan, you know."

Not exactly. Eitan tolerated his uncle and his attempts to offer fatherly advice. But Hank, bless his heart, worked long shifts as a fisherman, had four kids of his own to father, and a wife who made all of the parenting decisions.

Ma'ayan smiled into the phone to keep her voice light. "Thank you for the thought, but no. I support his decision."

Ma'ayan's phone buzzed to tell her another call was coming in—from Peter.

"Amit, I have to go. Important call on the other line. Give my love to the kids. Bye!"

Did it. Almost guiltless, too.

"Hi, Peter."

"Hey, pretty lady."

Ma'ayan's lips remembered last night's kiss. They started tingling even as they spoke with joking sarcasm, "What, another social SOS, is it?"

Peter laughed. "Nope. I'm asking you on a date. Just you and me. But it's not a normal date."

"Define abnormal."

"Have you ever shot a gun?"

"I live in Texas."

"You know the shooting range south of town?"

"Yes."

"Abnormal date: Meet me there at high noon tomorrow. Gotta run. Yes?"

"Well, I…"

"Good. See you then."

The call ended. Ma'ayan stared at her phone as she wandered into the kitchen. She set her empty coffee mug down and put two pieces of bread in the toaster.

What was it about that man? What did he want? Why did she trust him? Bingo. That was the biggest question. Ma'ayan barely trusted herself, let alone anyone else. Let alone a man.

Peter seemed to pull her out of herself. She looked at the time. Just after 9:00 a.m. Eitan would be telling his friends in first period about his trip to Israel. Amit would be calling their father and divulging the news Ma'ayan didn't want to reveal on an empty stomach.

The toast popped and she absentmindedly slathered each slice with butter and jam. There would be bagels for breakfast in Israel. Real bagels.

She brought the plate to her desk where her laptop had gone to sleep during the phone calls. She took a bite of toast, licked her fingers, and started the story that was taking her home.

•ן•

The next day, at noon, Ma'ayan slowed her Triumph as she pulled into the gravel parking lot of the shooting range. She parked close to the road beneath an oak tree. A few acorns from last fall mixed in with the gravel.

She stood looking across massive SUVs and trucks, most black and with rifle racks. She spotted Peter's modest, four-door sedan. It was the kind of car that blended in anywhere but a shooting range.

When Ma'ayan said she'd shot a gun before, she had told the truth. But it had only been once. A few years before, on a trip to visit her and Eitan, Ma'ayan's father had asked to bring her son here for some shooting practice.

She still remembered her father's thick, Israeli accent. "Boys should learn such skills. I had to serve three years in the Israeli Defense Force. You," he had pointed to her, "you would have had to serve two. You should come, too."

And so the grandfather-grandson bonding time turned into three generations of Bracha's unloading guns at targets.

Peter was waiting for Ma'ayan in the shop near the rifles. She smiled. "Going hunting?"

He turned and smiled back, leaning toward her to kiss

her on the cheek. When he pulled back, his eyes were asking a question Ma'ayan didn't think she could answer.

Instead, she smiled brightly. "Guess who's going to Israel?"

"Good. I'm glad to hear it."

"Eitan, too. He convinced me. He has that power."

Peter started moving toward the shooting gallery and placed his hand on Ma'ayan's back. "It's called favor. He walks in what his mother does."

"Favor? I guess." All Ma'ayan could think about was the feeling of the palm of his hand on her back. Stop it, she told herself. You're not eighteen any more.

Peter paid for their entry and handed Ma'ayan the obligatory safety glasses and earplugs.

Ma'ayan accepted them and looked up to find Peter watching her with a different look in his eyes. He said, "What is in you is greater than what you are living. Did you notice the oak tree in the parking lot?"

"Yes. I parked beneath it."

"The potential for the oak tree is already in the acorn. Most of us live like the acorn, forgetting we have an oak tree in us."

"Did you major in philosophy?"

"Minor." He pointed to her protective gear. "Put those on."

He led her outside to a long row of covered tables. From each table stretched out a lane, and at the end of each lane were targets. Most of the tables were full with lunchtime shooters.

Peter led them to a vacant table between a heavyset woman and a lithe man with wiry forearms. Peter set down his bag. Through the earplugs, his voice sounded distant. "Do you like Glocks?"

"Only with Tabasco."

He smiled and pulled out a matte black pistol, showing her the empty cartridge before handing it to her. "Feel how light it is."

She hadn't held one before. "It always amazes me that something so small can have so much power."

She looked from the gun to Peter, "It's the twenty-first century version of the acorn metaphor."

"I wasn't philosophizing, earlier."

Ma'ayan smiled. "And I wasn't mocking you. I was listening."

She handed the Glock back to him and continued as he began to load it. "Actually, I was deflecting, because I know you're right. I often feel that what I see of myself on the outside doesn't match up to what's inside."

Peter loaded and locked the gun. "And that's why you've been invited to write about us, Ma'ayan. I'm sharing some secrets of the Overcomers. We know that our argument with death is our unfinished assignment—that is why we have no fear. To truly overcome, you must become. You must first be who you truly are."

He sighted the gun, holding it with straight, still arms. When he broke form, he told her, "And it won't hurt to know how to shoot a gun where you're going. Do you know how to hold it?"

She carefully took the gun from him, keeping the barrel down and away from any and all limbs and organs.

He guided her arms, straightening her elbows, and showing her how to cradle her gun hand with the other. Then he stepped back. "Aim the sight at the target. Wherever the sight goes, the bullet goes."

"OK. And here I go."

She pulled the trigger and felt the recoil of the gun in her torso. She lowered the Glock and squinted into the distance. It looked like she'd hit one of the rings. She smiled

and turned to Peter to see what he thought. He wasn't
standing there. He was lying on the ground.

Ma'ayan froze. For a crazy second, she wondered if she
had shot him. But she'd only fired one bullet before lowering the gun. She placed it on the table as the overweight
woman next to them began screaming. A small, red spot
had appeared on Peter's white t-shirt.

Peter blinked and reached slowly toward his neck.
Ma'ayan knelt down as she yelled to the gathering crowd,
"Help, someone get help!"

The wiry man who had been at the table next to them
was gone.

Chapter Ten
Tel Aviv, Israel

JALIL DID NOT like this city. The traffic, the noise, the intensity. He sighed and his stomach growled. Maybe part of his mood was due to hunger.

His favorite place to get schwarma was nearby. His expression lightened at the thought. He entered beneath the sign depicting a stylized sun in bright yellow and orange. He waited at the counter next to a young Israeli man with a large machine gun casually hung over his civilian jacket.

When it was his turn, Jalil ordered a large schwarma, watching the man behind the counter shave turkey off of the three-foot spit with an electric saw.

Jalil blanched, remembering that morning.

Qisas—blood-wit. Jalil knew it had to happen, but that hadn't made watching it any easier. Two of Azzam's men had gotten drunk the night before. Alcohol was against the rules to start with. Then, one man had knocked out some of the other's teeth in a fistfight. The laws of blood-wit meant that the same teeth would be pulled out of the attacker in retribution.

Azzam held the Takbir to high standards. They were in the service of Allah; what higher standard was there?

Jalil wondered if he was the only one who doubted. No one ever admitted to anything other than enthusiastic support for the cause: Allah—and death to all infidels who didn't worship him.

Jalil sat at the counter, perpendicular to the street, looking at his lunch and trying to regain his appetite.

And now he had to tell his boss that the Overcomers knew about them, were probably ready for them. He had just overheard a conversation in the Uziel's garden.

He stood, his meal barely touched, and walked away.

This wasn't going to be a good day.

•ר•

Dr. Uziel's wife, a frail, widowed grandmother, gave Jason a hug so tight it almost hurt his ribs.

When she released him, her lined face was filled with gratitude. In English, she said, "Thank you for coming."

Jason removed his baseball cap and nodded. He hadn't had time to change into something more respectful, and he felt a bit awkward standing there in his jeans and t-shirt. No one seemed to notice.

Shafiq received the same warm welcome, and then Mrs. Uziel directed them to a table of food. During the seven-day Shiva, visitors and family came and went in constant, quiet streams. At the moment, a group sat quietly on the floor, near the mourning candle.

Mrs. Uziel stood by the men as they selected some Kosher cold cuts and nuts from the table. She held one hand with another and asked in a low voice, "Have you discovered anything?"

Jason and Shafiq exchanged glances.

Jason spoke. "A little. We know a new alliance has formed, and we know the OTF is one of their targets, but only on the way to something bigger. Do you know what your husband was working on before he died?"

Mrs. Uziel brought her folded hands to her chin in concentration. "Many things. He worked on so many things at the same time. We had been quite busy. Two of our grand-children had come from England to visit. We…" Her voice trailed off as the sadness of her husband's death found her again.

Her eyes began to water.

Shafiq put a hand on her shoulder. "Leo Uziel was one of the best men I knew."

She nodded and smiled, even as she wiped her eyes. "You may still ask me questions. I can help you and mourn at the same time."

Shafiq remembered something. "The Hebrew letter vav. Does that have any significance to you? Your husband was holding a piece of the newspaper when he died. He had circled the letter vav."

Mrs. Uziel tilted her head. "Vav. My husband knew the deep meanings of all the Hebrew letters. So many meanings. I know only a little, some of the basics. Vav means connection—connection between heaven and earth, God and man. Come. I will show you a book."

She led them out of the room, past a mirror draped in black. They passed through a hallway and emerged into a library brimming with books: books lining the walls, books in stacks of precarious height, books on the desk, books burying an arm chair. The room smelled of leather, old paper, and the faint sweetness of pipe tobacco.

Mrs. Uziel walked over to the shelf near the window, running her wrinkled fingers along leathered spines and squinting at the script on them.

"Here." She drew out a large tome and began flipping through it.

Finding the page she wanted, she put the book down on a pile of papers on the desk so the men could see.

"Vav." She pointed to the hook-shaped letter, presented in various forms of cursive and print.

"It represents the number six—the number of man. Hmmm. This letter is interesting. All Hebrew letters must be well-formed—not touching each other, or broken, or badly written. But the vav is an exception."

She scanned through the paragraphs of script. "It can sometimes be broken to represent the brokenness of man and our need for deliverance. It also represents the brokenness of the Mashiach—the Messiah—for that deliverance.

She silently read down the page. "In the Scriptures, the vav is broken in the word shalom, in the story of Phineas who brought atonement to Israel."

Mrs. Uziel stood up from the book. Light from the window cast her face in harsh, true light. "That is what Leo worked for. For Israel's deliverance. For understanding that could lead to peace. That is why he became one of you."

She walked toward the light coming through the window. The wrinkles on her face faded the closer she stood to its brightness. Without looking at the two men, she said, "You can know things that are to come. Leo sometimes did, but mostly he knew of things that had happened. He linked those to things that are to come."

She turned. "And you? Do either of you know what is coming?"

Jason nodded. "Sometimes."

Shafiq added, "And we know someone is coming who can help us."

Chapter Eleven

Fort Worth, Texas

S HE DREAMT OF an acorn. Its little cap lifted off, and out came a fully-formed, tiny oak tree. As the tree emerged, it grew larger and larger, so large its roots reached from Texas to Tel Aviv, and its leaves reached through the Earth's atmosphere into the heavens. The tree spoke: "Ask me, and I'll tell you the things you do not know."

Ma'ayan woke. The little red letters of her alarm read 3:33.

There was not even a brief second of waking without remembering Peter had died. His death seemed to have entered her life. She would not let his death be for nothing. But she couldn't build any strategy yet. Her head hurt. Her heart hurt. Just as she had begun to hope...

She surrendered to wakefulness and elbowed herself to a sitting position. In the dark, she tried to assemble the rest of yesterday.

The woman keeps screaming.

Peter's eyes find mine. He manages to lift his hand to his white stone necklace. "Your gift—your—power is for-giveness. Use it. Take this."

Staff clear the area. I'm holding his hand when he dies. He dies.

Tito comes with the local police. He prays over Peter, says something crazy about coming back to life. But I can see Nikki on his face. He looks like he's lost something.

Paramedics take Peter away. My friends in the force ask me questions. I remember the man next to us. Someone saw him leave. The girl behind the shop counter can describe him pretty well and saw him drive off.

Someone says there's hope we'll catch him. Hope? What use is that hope?

Ma'ayan broke her own reverie with a humorless laugh and got out of bed. She pulled on her robe and opened the French doors leading out to the back deck.

The spring night was clear and still. Out here on the edge of town, the stars were distinct and bright. Eitan could name many of the constellations. She smiled as she thought of her son. He had taken the news of Peter's death quietly, simply saying, "I'm sorry, Mom."

He'd given her a hug and sat with her in silence in the living room where, the night before, so much possibility had hung in the air. Neither of them said it, but they knew the trip was off.

But before that quiet close to the day had come another challenge: telling Peter's parents what had happened. They had come to the police station when she called Mike. Ma'ayan's instinct to call Peter's father had been a good one. His mother had gone into prompt hysterics, and it was a while before they arrived.

"Who? Who did this?" Elise kept asking of anyone who passed by.

Mike, ever stoic, kept his hand on his wife's shoulder.

Morgan, the toughest looking of the Texan Overcomers Ma'ayan had met, surprised her with his gentle compassion for Elise. He asked if he could bless her. At first she railed at him, yelling, "I don't want your blessing, I want my son back!"

He knelt down in front of her. Puzzled, Elise stopped crying.

Morgan extended his hand and repeated his question, "May I say a blessing over you and your family?"

Sniffling, Elise nodded, grabbing her husband's hand.

The words had been simple. In fact, Ma'ayan couldn't even remember them. But she remembered the feeling they left. It was as if the entire atmosphere of the police station—with all the heaviness that crossed its floors every day—had lifted. As if fresh air swirled through the residue of pain. As if, by kneeling on the floor where hopeless feet had trod, Morgan had released a freedom people would feel when they walked across those floors.

Ma'ayan's own heaviness shifted for a moment as she remembered that blessing. But it returned when she recalled the last part. Morgan had asked Elise to forgive the man. Elise had given a half nod. Or maybe it was just her head snapping in a startled reaction.

Forgive. That was a tall order to ask a mother hours after she lost her son. Ma'ayan didn't even know if she could forgive Peter's killer, and she had only recently met him. Had just started to fall for him.

She sighed at the stars. Peter's last words about the acorn had turned into a dream. She knew she was missing something—some vital part of her own life that was actually already within her. So really, she wasn't missing that something; she just wasn't using it.

What was it? Was it the part of her that could remain calm in the middle of chaos? The part that could strategize even as her emotions wanted to call it quits and have a good cry?

She hadn't cried. She'd put everything on hold. That was more exhausting than releasing the emotions, but she had grown good at maintaining equilibrium.

Yawning, she walked back into her room. As she turned out the light, she remembered Yola's words from a couple of days ago: With me, you overcome all. The word *with* repeated itself in her head until she fell asleep.

Azzam stood at his office window on the second floor, remembering his time as a young radical in the Iranian Revolution. The Ayatollah had advocated revolt and martyrdom against anything that came in the way of Shia Islam. That meant reversing the Westernization encouraged by the secular Shah. Azzam had been drilled with the Gharbzadegi mindset: Western culture was an infection to be cured with whatever means possible—his own death included, if need be. Islam would liberate the world from the ills of capitalism and colonialism. Such pure faith would be the world's only salvation.

Today, a fight had gotten in the way of purity. Azzam hated it when his men quarreled, especially the computer technicians. They didn't know how to fight, so they made more of a mess.

The late afternoon light turned the desert to a shimmering gold. Azzam had founded the Takbir years ago, out in a similar desert in Iran. For so long the group had been a secret. Azzam had wanted to wait to reveal the group's existence with the release of the virus. But his enthusiastic men had been too impatient—wanted the acknowledgement. He shrugged. So now they were known. So be it.

He thought of Hamas and their slogan: "We love death more than you love life." He preferred the Takbir's slogan. It had come to him one night in a dream. It began with the praise chant it was named for, but took it further: "Allah is the Greatest! All will acknowledge Allah or die!"

During the Revolution, people had shouted the original takbir from rooftops. The chant had echoed in Azzam's heart ever since. Soon, it would echo in the hearts of every living man and woman.

And the next step would be keeping this tiny nation from getting too excited about their natural gas discovery. Azzam smiled, remembering how he'd had to convince his men to wait until the Israelis had finished building the drilling platform before destroying it. They were still learning patience.

Azzam had certainly been patient about dealing with the Overcomers. He'd known about them for a while, but he had waited to begin targeting them until he felt close enough to wipe them out entirely. Meanwhile, it was gratifying to pick them off slowly—along with any other pet projects their American sponsor, Mr. Wexler, had planned.

Azzam turned from the window and looked at the photos on his desk. So many of them—and these were just the ones they'd found. The Overcomers were the only enemies he truly worried about. They too believed in their God. They too knew they had powers more potent than nuclear warfare.

But if belief meant power, Azzam couldn't imagine anyone having more power than he did. Allah burned in his being. He embodied Allah.

All would acknowledge Allah or die.

Chapter Twelve
Fort Worth, Texas

ELLA'S OWL WASN'T an oil painting hanging in a gilded frame like the Wexler's. Hers was a stuffed owl—a children's toy hanging in the arch leading to the living room. Ma'ayan hadn't paid attention to the owl the first time she came because of the riot of things everywhere. Della's collection was eccentric to say the least.

That eccentricity expressed itself most fully in her wardrobe. This evening, she was wearing what looked like a dozen shades of white and cream. Ma'ayan felt slightly odd dressed in black. Wasn't this a wake?

Della, as if seeing the confusion on Ma'ayan's face, stuck her finger in the air. "I got somethin' for you. Here. She pulled a white scarf from a basket near the door and wound it around Ma'ayan's neck and shoulders.

Della smiled. There you go. "We're celebrating Peter's life."

The room was full to bursting. All of the Overcomers from the last gathering were there, as well as Peter's parents and what Ma'ayan assumed were more of Peter's friends and family. The Wexler's were there, too. You could tell the Overcomers from the friends and family— the latter also wore black but had been draped with a scarf. The Overcomers were already head-to-toe in some shade of white.

Della clapped her hands. "This here's a celebration, so get yourself a drink, and I'm gonna make a toast."

Yola was making rounds with a large platter of champagne glasses. She came to Ma'ayan and whispered, "I've got something for you."

Ma'ayan accepted a glass of golden bubbles and started to ask what, but Yola was already serving someone else.

Despite the chaos of the previous day, despite being draped in a white scarf in a room half filled with crazies and half filled with really, really sad people, Ma'ayan felt like she had entered a safe house. The comfort here exceeded the grief. It was like Della's entire home was an heirloom quilt, well-worn about the seams from years of wrapping people up in its warmth.

Della stood at the entrance to the living room and clinked one of her many rings on her champagne glass, "OK, y'all. Make a big, thick circle. I'm gonna give a preachy toast, so get ready."

Laughter wove through the gathering circle.

Della, satisfied everyone was poised to listen, began: "In the beginning of the Scriptures, back when God was just startin' to create this holy mess of an earth, it says that the evening and the morning were the first day. Now why would God start day the night before? I'll tell you why. 'Cause every new beginning starts way before the light comes on. It starts in the darkness. In First Kings, the Lord said He'd dwell in the thick of darkness. That darkness is terrible. Peter's death was terrible. For sure, we can mourn—even when I make you wear some white scarf and call this a party."

Della shook her head as if to contradict herself, "But! But! Hear me: It's in the darkness that we find ourselves. All those everyday distractions go poof when somethin' terrible happens. We find ourselves alone with God. We find our night vision gettin' tuned. Psalm 134 says that by night we stand in the house of the Lord. This is our night watch mandate."

She swept the circle with her gaze. "Don't waste this sorrow. Don't waste this opportunity to see clearer, to fight better. I just dare you to live as a stronger light in this darkness. Remember, the darker it gets, the more you shine. We were born for this hour.

Della lifted up her glass. "Here's to this hour!"

The group lifted their glasses and clinked with those within arm's reach.

But Della wasn't done. As people sipped, she continued, "When we face problems, we can't rely on ourselves for the answers. Problems stay problems when we don't ask for heavenly answers. We gotta pull on heaven." Della, yanked down an imaginary chunk of the living room air.

Looking up at her hand, she saw the stuffed owl. She pulled it off its hook and held it high. "We see in the dark like the owl."

She closed her eyes, "Lord, give us eyes to see in the dark."

It happened again: the sense that an atmosphere had shifted. It was different than the police station because Della's house was already chock-full of peace. But people had brought their heaviness with them, and it lifted. Just like opening all the windows on a spring day after a cold, long winter when the air had grown stale without you noticing.

Ma'ayan took a deep breath. Randomly, she thought, I want to keep this scarf. It seemed symbolic of choosing a perspective of light.

Standing still in that peace, Della closed her eyes and leaned back her head. "Acts 9 strength, Lord. Acts 9. Give us Ananias eyes to see the future. An Ananias heart to obey the instructions we don't understand. An Ananias 'yes' to all that You ask of us."

Relatives and friends of Peter, whom Ma'ayan didn't know, looked a bit uncomfortable, started to exchange glances. The Overcomers started to space themselves around the circle.

Then Della slammed her hand on her ample thigh. "Open our eyes!"

And then it happened. It was as if the spirit realm collided with the physical. No—they became the same. Ma'ayan could see an open vision of herself and Eitan arriving in Tel Aviv, a man extending his hand toward her, a crowd gathering. She saw the scenarios simultaneously, though she knew they would unfold in time. They were going to happen—she knew this with an inexplicable sense of certainty. The vision stopped almost as soon as it started.

Ma'ayan realized she was sweating. Her heart was beating faster. As she looked around the room, she could see the others had experienced something similar. Looks of doubt were now a timid awe. What had just happened?

Laughing, Della nodded at everyone. "Yes. Yes. He'll show you the things you don't know. When He shows you the future, you come back to the present and walk it out." She snapped her fingers, "Confirm, my friends."

One at a time, the Overcomers stepped out of the circle and begin speaking to the visitors.

Tito told Peter's father, Mike, "Your prayer of last night will be answered."

Jesse Mae told Elise, "You will give birth to a dream you've had since grade school. The secret one."

Morgan laid his hand on Peter's brother and told him, "I see restoration going back generations. What was stolen from your forefathers will be restored through you. Walk in the favor and power and anointing that is yours by birth."

Each Overcomer shared something that only the person they were speaking to could know and then revealed an aspect of their calling. Watching the facial reactions, Ma'ayan found her emotions trying to slip out in the form of tears.

Finally, Yola popped into the middle with a smile and pointed at Ma'ayan. "Girl, you are going to Israel. No buts about it. You're gonna visit the good guys—and the bad guys. God tells you stuff in dreams. Start paying attention to them; they will be your assignments."

Ma'ayan nodded, thinking Yola had given her the "something" mentioned earlier.

But Yola continued. "Did you ever play Monopoly?"

"Yes." Ma'ayan had. She had been her household champion. Eitan had inherited her talent for it when he was little. The two of them could never get anyone else to join them because their games would go on forever.

"Remember the Get Out of Jail Free card?"

"Of course."

Yola dimpled and handed her an ordinary, white business card. "Think of this as a Get Out of Hell Free card."

Ma'ayan's brow wrinkled involuntarily at the mention of hell. Her mind jumped from childhood memories of a board game to medieval depictions of a fiery lake. Hesitating, she accepted the card. A single phone number was typeset into the front: an international number with an Israeli country code.

Yola was watching her. "If you run into any trouble there, he'll help. He knows you're coming."

Chapter Thirteen

Tel Aviv, Israel

MRS. LIYA BRACHA was hanging her laundry on the lines that ran across one side of her small garden.

Tomorrow. Tomorrow she is coming!

If only Liya's husband, Joseph, were still alive. Like her, he hadn't seen Ma'ayan since she left at age eight. All those decades. Amit had come back once. Liya loved Amit, of course. But Ma'ayan. Ma'ayan had been her soul mate and the only one who had seen through the steel façade that had kept Liya alive through war and rumors of war. Even Joseph, wonderful as he had been, did not have her blood in his veins like Ma'ayan did.

At ninety-two, Liya still did her own laundry and made her own hummus. She had done both on a grander scale today, rewashing the sheets on the guest beds and making enough hummus to feed four generations. One thing about age: Liya knew her limits. She'd asked her neighbor's daughter, Miriam, to come and help with the Passover cooking.

Liya had never met her grandson, Eitan. Oh, she hoped he wouldn't be one of those American boys with ear thingies and messy hair and no shoelaces. She'd seen the television shows.

But nothing mattered so much as seeing Ma'ayan again. Liya had been praying for both of her granddaughters since the days they were born. And tomorrow, thirty-something years after watching two little girls walk out of this garden with her son toward another land, Liya would see the shape half of those prayers had taken.

A small breeze slivered through the olive tree. The sleeves of her drying shirts began to reach out.

Tomorrow.

FORT WORTH, TEXAS

Another dawn was breaking over a Texan highway, but this time Ma'ayan wasn't on her Triumph, and Eitan was with her.

Victor's driver wore a hat. "Just like in the movies," Eitan had whispered when they slid in the back seat into a world of leather seats and surround sound.

A large envelope lay in the middle of the back seat. From the front, the driver said, "Something for you from the Wexler's."

Ma'ayan had been holding it, indulging in the peace of the Bentley's interior after a few days of laundry, phone calls, and paperwork.

Eitan finally elbowed her, "Hey, shouldn't you open it before we get to the airport?"

"Right. Any guesses? Microchip? Mystery address and old photo? GPS coordinates?"

"I'm thinking flash drive and a letter."

"Hmmm." Ma'ayan tore off the top of the envelope and pulled a letter and a sleek, tiny flash drive with almost as much memory as her computer.

In an exaggerated Israeli accent, Ma'ayan told her son: "You so smart!"

Together, they read the letter:

Dear Ma'ayan,

I'm sure you remember meeting Jesse Mae at Della's house. She had another dream, based on Psalm 83, about how the nations desire to oppress Israel. They did when Asaph wrote that Psalm, and they desire to do so today. Alliances are forming that could have destructive powers like those that have been prophesied. And though prophecies are meant to come true, their expression can look different if we play our parts.

Your part is vital. You were made for this time, this assignment. Don't underestimate the magnitude of the task before you. You're not just going to Israel to document the Overcomers; you are going to Israel to overcome. And you can't do this alone.

Invite revelation in your dreams. Jesse Mae says you'll receive instruction. You've seen enough to know there's something in all of this—strange as it can appear. Your gift of questioning and skepticism serves you well to get to the heart of a story but not to get to your own heart. Trust that the God who created the universe can surprise you now and then.

Give the flash drive to the man who picks you up at the Ben Gurion Airport.

Thank you for helping to save a nation.

Shalom,

Victor and Karla Wexler

The airport terminal was suddenly in front of them. The driver slowed to a stop and climbed out to open Ma'ayan's door before going to the trunk. Eitan leapt out to help him.

"Thank you," Ma'ayan said to the driver as she fished around in her purse for her wallet. How much should she give him?

The driver was tipping his hat and shaking his head. "I'm well taken care of, ma'am. Have a good journey."

He was in the car before she could protest.

Ma'ayan sighed. "Well, here we go." She started to gather her bags, wondered if she was forgetting anything. Instead of remembering her list, something else popped into her mind—part of Della's prayer. Aloud she asked, "Ananias. Who the heck is Ananias?

Eitan picked up his suitcase. "Who?"

As if on cue, a dusty, rusty red Volkswagen came careening to the curb. It huffed to a stop, and Della not so much climbed as heaved herself out. "Ma'ayan!"

Ma'ayan and Eitan set down their bags as Della bolted toward them, a white scarf curving behind her like a veil. "I got somethin' for you."

Ma'ayan smiled. "I did like that scarf."

Della, wiping a bit of sweat from her upper lip, chuckled and shook her head. "I knew it. You got a minute?"

Without waiting for an answer, Della continued. "I woke up this morning dang early with somethin' to tell you. Hoped I could just call you, but God said, 'Nope. You get yourself to the airport and say it with that scarf.' So here I am."

She started winding the scarf around Ma'ayan's neck. "This here's a declaration for you. You're going to God's country, literally. You give Him your abilities, and He'll give you favor."

Della lowered her voice to a whisper, "Favor is the secret. That's one of the gifts the Overcomers have, Ma'ayan. They know they walk in God's favor, and they don't waste it. The more they use their gift, the more He gives them. Your enemies don't like that. But remember: God's a whole lot bigger than anybody—good or evil. Partner with that goodness and you'll crush the evil."

"And you," she turned to Eitan with a smile. He was watching her with a furrowed brow. "You got a destiny on you so big nobody would believe it. But you know it. You know there's somethin' so deep in you that's gotta come out. You have an idea how, but be prepared."

Della started laughing loudly, "Oh, yes! Be prepared! Now shoo, you two. Those lines are gettin' long."

And without waiting for a response, Della bounced back to her car, waved furiously from behind the dusty windshield, and pulled away.

Eitan looked at his mother.

She winked. "Call it coincidence."

Chapter Fourteen

Havilah Gas Field, Mediterranean Sea
In the waters of the Israeli
exclusive economic zone (EEZ)

ABOVE, THE AZURE sky stretched from one horizon of sea to the next. Below—5,000 feet below—waited billions and billions of cubic meters of natural gas. They had found it. Zadok held the railing and breathed the salty air deep into his lungs.

Twenty years of his life he had spent believing in this. Twenty years of believing that this might help fulfill an ancient prophecy.

Golda Meir, bless her heart, hadn't helped that belief. She unintentionally set a mindset of impossibility when she famously said as Israeli prime minister, "Let me tell you something that we Israelis have against Moses. He took us forty years through the desert in order to bring us to the one spot in the Middle East that has no oil." Or gas, for that matter. Israel had been completely dependent on foreign fuel.

Zadok had been in the Israeli Defense Force when he heard that. He had believed it, like most everyone else.

He'd gone on to university, earned a business degree, and ended up working in investment real estate in Tel Aviv for a couple of decades before he heard that quote again. He had been forty then, helping his son with his Bible homework. One morning before breakfast, they had been studying the passages in Ezekiel describing the wealth that Israel would one day have.

Zadok had driven his son to school and stopped at a gas station on the way home. As he filled his tank, he had, what he has since described to skeptical investors as, a vision. He saw pipes rising from Israeli waters spewing gas.

Drilling in the Mediterranean: that would make Israel's neighbors even more unhappy about his homeland than they already were. But the idea had caught hold of him. He knew he had to bring it to life.

Only a few investors had felt the thrill of his vision. They had been willing to risk not just their finances but also their reputations. Most investors with Arab clients didn't want to risk annoying them.

Now, far from land on a drilling platform he had helped to design, the vision Zadok had seen while standing next to his car's fuel tank had taken the shape of an industrial floating structure poised to bring unparalleled wealth to his tiny country.

Zadok's phone rang. He smiled at the number and answered, "Mr. Wexler. We're ready to begin."

•ן•

Far below, the Mediterranean lay out in a slab of blue. Ma'ayan had won the window seat on the argument that she could never sleep on planes and liked to watch the sky. That, and Eitan took the window on the first leg of the trip.

She squinted: Was that a ship? No, some offshore station. What a life to work out in the middle of water. She stretched. Wasn't her thing. Give her land any day.

Ma'ayan's notebook lay open across her closed laptop. She'd spent much of the flight filling the paper book with single words and sketches and lots of linking lines formed of sentence fragments.

She had saved several documents to her laptop before leaving—documents about the history of the nation of Israel and Middle Eastern conflicts.

The purser's voice came over the first-class speakers: "We have entered Israeli airspace. Please return to your seats."

Eitan turned and rubbed his eyes. "Are we close?"

"Yep. And something tells me Safta Liya has been cooking food since dawn."

"Good, I'm starving."

"You're the one who told me not to wake you for meal service, mister."

Eitan smiled and scratched his head. His hair stuck out at every geometric angle.

Ma'ayan reached over to smooth it and said, "I'd take sleep over plane food any day. First class or not."

She wadded up her blanket and kicked an in-flight magazine out of the way. Her teeth felt furry and her clothes sticky.

The plane landed on time, and passengers began their slow procession through long hallways and lines. Ben Gurion Airport was spacious and full of light, and the Arrivals passageway recalled a well-designed museum of antiquities.

Eitan's eyes widened a bit at the men in uniform with large machine guns. Ma'ayan felt an odd pull of past and present—almost as if her shorter, eight-year-old self were trying to grow into her current adult height and experiences. That tension, combined with lack of sleep and the remembrance of everything that had brought her here, made Ma'ayan's eyes sting for a threatening second with tears.

She smiled them away and kept moving. Customs and baggage claim were relatively painless. In less than an hour after landing, Ma'ayan and Eitan found themselves entering the packed greeting area. A line of drivers held signs with handwritten and printed names. One held up an electronic tablet with Hebrew script that Ma'ayan was too far away to read.

Victor said their driver would know them, but a sign would have been nice. Eitan kept close, and so Ma'ayan thought it was his hand that touched her shoulder as they were halfway through the crowd. She turned and found herself looking directly into the solid face of a stranger, his arm extending toward her through the crowd. She froze. It was the man from her vision.

He smiled at her. "You are Ma'ayan, the one sent to write about us?"

Ma'ayan's blood started flowing again. "Yes."

"My name is Shafiq. I will be driving you."

He didn't look like Victor's driver in Fort Worth. This guy looked like he only drove vehicles that were big and loaded with things that went "boom."

Eitan saw it first. "You're wearing the stone."

Of course, Ma'ayan thought.

Shafiq was looking at her son. He kept looking, as if he saw far more than a young man from America who liked to write computer code and cook his mom dinner. Shafiq looked at him with the look Jesse Mae had given Ma'ayan when she described the daisy pen.

The silence grew, but Shafiq was obviously not done with whatever thought or spirit process moved through him.

Finally, he put a hand on Eitan's shoulder and said, "You will wear one someday, too."

ARIEL, ISRAEL

Azzam stood next to the computer technician. The man was young enough to be Azzam's son, and he clearly looked at Azzam as a father figure. With a large smile and a gangly wave, he called out when he saw his leader, "Please, sir. Come and see this."

Azzam came to stand next to Shahkam.

Shahkam, who spent most of his time in front of a screen, spoke rapidly when faced with a human, "The Russian codes worked. The infected systems have downloaded our virus." The young man's eyes glowed. "We have real-time control over the trial systems."

Azzam looked at the computer screen. He didn't know what the numbers and letters meant individually, but he knew what they would mean for the Takbir. For the world.

Azzam asked, "This control, is it remote?"

Shahkam's head bobbed up and down, his enthusiasm exploding like an opened soda can. "Yes. You can access it from any commercial Internet access. We can search and download any file, open any device—webcams, microphones. Unless we want them to, no one will know. Of course, most people know not to open an unknown link, so we have created a trial web page with an exploit code that infects the computers of anyone who visits that page."

Shahkam did a quick search for a photo of the Prime Minister. His face filled the screen. Shakham pointed to him, "Say you target the Prime Minister. Once his computer is infected, it will check in with our control server. We send instructions to download and install our virus. The Prime Minister's computer will keep working fine—no crashing. Meanwhile, we access all of his contacts..."

Azzam pursed his lips. It was hard to tell if he was smiling. "And the Takbir virus is born."

Shahkam lowered his voice. "Sir, you said you would let

us know what website you wanted. It can look like government, non-profit—anything you like."

Azzam crossed his arms. This time his smile was unmistakable. "You know, I long ago learned to make use of existing resources. We will counterfeit an existing site, a Pro-Israeli site that already has users and traffic. You have heard of it: Arabs for Israel."

Shahkam's face spread with joyful awe as he turned back to his computer. The unchanged face of the Prime Minister watched him from the screen.

Chapter Fifteen

Tel Aviv, Israel

THE CAR SHAFIQ drove was not a Bentley. If there had been shocks in the old Sabra, they had gone the way of the paint job. As the three rattled from the airport toward the city, the warm wind sliced through the open windows.

Eitan sprawled across the back seats, looking right and left. In the front, Ma'ayan let her hair slap her face. The sting of it seemed to ground her.

Shafiq patted the steering wheel. "Sorry for the car. I borrowed it. You know what a Sabra is?"

Ma'ayan nodded. "The cactus fruit. Prickly outside, sweet inside."

"Yes. Also, it is the name of this car and the nickname for native-born Israelis." He smiled. "Thankfully most of the Israelis are in better shape than this car."

Ma'ayan smiled. He wasn't as gruff as he looked, and he looked like he enjoyed wrestling tanks. She asked, "I may be native born, but I don't know if I'm a Sabra. Too much America." She paused. "You know the way to my grandmother's house?"

"Yes. But we're stopping somewhere else first." He turned toward her and added, "Don't worry; I told Mrs. Bracha. I had grandmothers, too."

Ma'ayan wasn't sure if he was being funny or pensive. She wondered how this Arab man became an Overcomer, what his story was, where he called home.

Home. As they neared the city, so much looked different and so much the same. Everything was bigger, but not because Ma'ayan had grown. The buildings in the distance were taller—and there were more of them. More traffic, too.

Shafiq turned down an old, industrial street on the edge of the city. Buildings of crumbly cement labeled with faded signs stood next to renovated business fronts with brightly painted letters and numbers. Street-level shop fronts were crammed with auto repair, electronics, and computers.

Eitan leaned forward as Shafiq slowed the Sabra and squeezed it diagonally into half a parking space. They had stopped in front of one of the crumbling buildings. The shop window was filled with computers, wires, and a black cat sitting on top of them.

The cat looked up when the three walked in, flicked its tail, and readjusted its head on its front paws.

Shafiq led them into the dim back of the shop, where a tall, thin man was stooped over a disassembled tablet.

The man looked up and smiled; in Arabic he said, "Peace be upon you."

Shafiq nodded, "And also upon you, Muhammed Khan."

Eitan had already started examining the guts of a PC, its parts splayed out across a table.

Shafiq turned and gestured to Ma'ayan, "She has come."

The man stood and looked hopefully at Ma'ayan. "She brought it?"

Without understanding what the men were saying, Ma'ayan had already guessed what they were doing here. She reached into her purse and pulled out the envelope Victor's driver had given her.

Israeli Security Agency (Shin Bet) Tel Aviv

It was a good day in the Shin Bet's Technology Division. Rebekah had made a trial batch of semolina cake for Passover and brought it to the office. The largely male division was in the process of critique:

"Just like my safta's. Bless her heart, she didn't know how to bake."

"Maybe too much lemon."

"No, more lemon."

"Can I have another piece?"

Rebekah laughed and shooed her coworkers away. "Hurry. The boss will be through soon."

Karl, the thickest of the Division staff, grabbed another piece and said, "Maybe you should save him a piece."

"You know he doesn't like sweets—or me bringing them. Go!" Rebekah waved them away, bundling up the remains of the cake in her canvas market bag and stashing the evidence at her feet.

Rebekah wiped her hands on her slacks and reached for her keyboard. She liked her job. She like analyzing data, especially when she discovered insecure, web-based interfaces—weak links hackers could use to communicate with compromised computers. If average computer users with Internet access had any idea how vulnerable their systems were... She sighed. Well, that was what she was there for.

She was proud she had helped avert cyber disasters. The Shin Bet information systems had helped prevent untold terrorist attacks. And more than once, her team had helped stopped an attack just as the terrorist had arrived at the planned site. It was all about paying attention and timing.

"I heard a rumor."

Rebekah looked up to find her boss, Mr. Ben-Ami, trying not to smile.

"Let me guess. About semolina cakes? Ah, you must have false information, sir."

He looked at her desk. "Must have. No visible evidence to support the rumor."

Rebekah pursed her lips and shook her head in mock seriousness. "And one must have evidence." She sighed and rested her chin on her hand. "But rest assured, the evidence in question wouldn't be very useful. It likely had too much lemon."

Mr. Ben-Ami was trying not to smile again. "Well, in that case, I wouldn't be tempted to analyze it."

He gave a curt nod and continued down the hall.

Rebekah sighed again. If only her semolina cakes were as reliable as her programming. Then she smiled. It was kind of nice to have a few insignificant problems when you spent the day trying to save the world from terrorism.

She glanced at her clock. Time for a moment of fresh air…and the chance to make a call. One of the drawbacks to working in a high security facility: no calls from private phones in the office.

She grabbed her smart phone and headed for the doors. Outside, the warm spring wind sent her red curls flying. As she started to call, her phone rang.

Smiling, she answered it. "Shalom, Jason."

"She's here."

"And tonight?"

"Yes, we meet."

Chapter Sixteen

RUSH HOUR IN Tel Aviv was a synonym for "parking lot." It was dark before Shafiq drove into the neighborhood where Ma'ayan had spent the first years of her life. The tiredness that had begun to settle in her bones on the drive lifted as the familiar streets curved into view. And then there was her grandmother's house—inside lights all blazing and garden lights reaching into the street.

Before the rattling Sabra had fully shuttered to a stop, Liya Bracha was reaching to open the passenger door, her smile crinkling her face in lines of joy.

Ma'ayan's smile was just as big as she climbed out of the car. "Safta!"

She had to bend over slightly to hug her grandmother. As they embraced, the decades fell away. Standing next to her safta, Ma'ayan was both the adult of now and the girl of once. Time stood still, even as it leapt backward and forward. Ma'ayan could see her childhood in this house unfurling like a film, overlaid with events of the months to come.

The sensation of timelessness rose and fell away so quickly, Ma'ayan wasn't even sure she had felt it. The feeling that did remain was a sense of completeness that she had forgotten was possible. There, in her grandmother's arms, Ma'ayan remembered who she was.

As Ma'ayan released her grandmother, she also felt something familiar about her—something Ma'ayan had encountered recently. But she was forgetting Eitan.

She stood back and reached for her son, "And this is your great-grandson, Eitan."

Eitan stepped forward, his smile slightly shy and respectful. He bent over even farther to hug Liya, who was talking all the while in Hebrew. He looked over his great-grandmother's shoulder at his mother and mouthed, "I can't understand her."

When Liya finally released Eitan, Ma'ayan gently spoke English, "Safta, Eitan doesn't speak Hebrew."

Eitan added, "Not yet. But I want to learn."

Ma'ayan looked at him, "Really? You never told me that. I would have taught you."

Eitan smiled. "I didn't know I wanted to. But I do like my heritage. That's why I kept the Bracha name."

Liya was watching mother and son. "Hebrew I can teach. Love of Israel? No. But you already have that. Best way to start." She slapped Eitan on his back with a force that surprised him.

Ma'ayan shook her head with a smile and saw Shafiq. They had forgotten him. He was standing near the driver's door, watching the reunion without expression. He seemed perfectly fine waiting.

Ma'ayan reached in the car for her purse. "Oh, I'm sorry. We're probably keeping you. We'll get the bags."

Shafiq walked to the back of the car. "I will bring them."

Liya nodded, "Come. I have something to show you."

Ma'ayan and Eitan followed the spry, old woman through the garden and into the house. They entered a tiled hall and heard voices. When they turned the corner into the living room, it was to find it full of people.

Liya clapped her hands together. "Welcome to Israel!"

Two things struck Ma'ayan at once. The sense of familiarity she'd felt as she hugged her grandmother was because Liya reminded her of Della—which was confirmed by the other thing: almost everyone in her safta's living room was wearing a white stone necklace.

OLD JAFFA, ISRAEL

"When your building stands in one of the oldest cities in the world, you've got to expect to make a few improvements." Margie was giving her husband that look he'd learned to translate within three days of their now thirty-year marriage.

Ruben sighed. She was right, but one, he didn't want to admit that, and two, he didn't consider new windows to be worth the contractor's quote. He had better places to spend this money. So did his wife.

"Margie, we'll be late."

"My love, 'late' to you is 'on time' to the rest of the world. Or at least the rest of the staff. Just look."

She held the catalog toward her husband. "These would look good; they fit with the historical integrity of the stone and the Jaffa blue."

Ruben pulled out his glasses and looked at the windows his wife had selected. "They look very nice."

She slammed the catalog shut. "Oh, you know very well that's no answer. Of course they look very nice. I'm asking if we can order them."

Ruben pulled his glasses off again, a glimmer in his eyes. "You want windows more than the sailing trip, eh?"

Margie smiled a large, glowering, smile. "Both/and, my dear. Both/and."

Ruben threw his hands in the air and headed for the door. "I'll be in the car."

Margie lifted her purse onto her shoulder and started to follow her husband. Aloud to the old windows, she said with a smile, "I'm sure you're just as tired of us as we are of you. Don't worry, you'll retire soon. I'll win."

Chapter Seventeen
Havilah Gas Field, Mediterranean Sea

ZADOK STEPPED INSIDE to avoid the noise of the drill. Victor Wexler's voice on the satellite phone sounded tense. "One of our intercessors warned us of an upcoming danger. She couldn't see what it was exactly. Not natural disaster. Man-made."

Zadok started walking along primary-colored pipes, past the control room and a rack of hard hats. He said, "I'll ask my people here."

Victor sighed. "Thank you, Z. We're not going to be defeated at this point. Oh, and Jessie Mae said to bless the skies."

Zakok paused, his boots sticking to the plank grating walkway. "Do you think there's a missile attack planned?"

Victor laughed without humor. "You're the one who lives in Israel, Z."

Zadok smiled into the phone, "True. That is one of the good things about working out here on the Sea. Less chance of death by bomb."

"Well, maybe not."

The thin humor drained from both men at the same moment.

Rallying, Zadok said, "If we are helping to fulfill a prophecy, then we keep doing what we're doing. In fact, perhaps the sign that we're on the right track is the threat of attack."

"I wonder if terrorists feel the same way?"

Zadok looked up through the multi-leveled facility. Everywhere one looked there were pipes of all sizes and colors. Pipes that would help bring raw materials from great depths to the surface. They were in the business of bridging distance. Distance of space and time. Distance between prophecy and fulfillment. Distance between light and dark.

In his constant laps around the outer perimeter of the facility, Zadok always felt not just the shifts in natural atmosphere but the spiritual ones as well.

He remembered he was still on the phone. "Probably. But our goal is bloodless wealth for Israel, not blood for blood."

Victor's voice reached from the United States to the Mediterranean, as if it gained power with each mile, "I bless you and your family, my friend."

"And blessings to you and yours."

Zadok hung up, glad there was no distance in the spirit.

Tel Aviv, Israel

Ma'ayan caught Eitan's eye over a plate heaped high with hummus, grated beet salad, and pita bread. She whispered, "You know how long this day was? This is the day we flew here from Texas."

Eitan whispered back, "Technically, that was yesterday, Mom."

"Really? Without sleep, I can't tell."

Ma'ayan felt a tap on her shoulder. She turned to see Ishay smiling at her. "Thank you for coming."

Ma'ayan smiled back. "It is good to be here—both to work and to be back home."

Liya emerged from the kitchen bearing a tray of reinforcements: olives, soft cheese, and more mint tea.

"Safta, let me get that," Ma'ayan reached for the heavy

tray, but Liya shrugged her away—deftly managing not to spill anything.

Liya slid the tray into a spot at the end of the table and straightened. "You know the story of Caleb? He had the strength of a forty-year-old at eighty-five. I asked God for that. Caleb needed his strength to fight wars with spears and shields. I need it to fight dirt and an empty refrigerator."

Ishay laughed. "I don't believe her refrigerator is ever empty."

A man came up for a glass of mint tea. "I do believe that when we get to heaven, it will be largely populated by praying grandmothers."

He smiled at Liya and then looked at Ma'ayan, extending his hand, "Shalom. I am Jason Wexler. And this is my girlfriend, Rebekah."

A lovely woman with auburn hair and freckles stepped forward to shake Ma'ayan's hand. "I have been waiting to meet you. Thank you for coming. Thank you for coming to Israel."

Ma'ayan was starting to wonder what it was that everyone expected of her. This entire welcoming committee to write a few stories?

Like his father, Jason Wexler seemed to be slightly telepathic. He smiled at her. "Don't worry, this gathering happens every week. We just coordinated this week's meeting with your arrival."

Ishay nodded. "We'll all be gone before the jet lag kicks in."

Ma'ayan set down her plate and smiled. "Well that's a relief." She reached for her purse and took out her notebook and a pen. "I may as well take notes. Let's start with our definitions. The public doesn't know much, if anything, about you all, correct?"

"Correct."

"So. If I were to do an online search, what definition would you want to pop up for the Overcomers?"

Jason looked around the room. "I think that's a perfect cue to begin. Liya?"

She nodded and clapped her hands, speaking in Hebrew to the gathering. Ma'ayan had to concentrate, but her native language was still there, tucked deep beneath decades of primarily speaking English. She was glad that her father had mostly spoken Hebrew to her and her sister after their move to the United States.

The small gathering found places on sofas and ottomans and the lush Persian carpet in the center of a large expanse of cool, stone floors.

Liya was indeed the Israeli version of Della. She even told everyone to get some mint tea before they began. Ma'ayan had flashbacks to her first Overcomer meeting in Texas with sweet tea. The displacement was actually pleasant; whether it was that or the jet lag, Ma'ayan felt open to a new level of awareness here.

Liya was speaking in Hebrew and then stopped herself. "Ah, Eitan still must learn this language. Can we speak in English tonight?"

Heads nodded. A man raised his hand. Liya nodded, "Of course," even as she began pulling him to a standing position.

He laughed. "This woman could beat me in an elbow wrestling match."

Eitan whispered to his mother, "Do they elbow wrestle in Israel?" She nudged him hard in the ribs and tried not to smile.

The man who stood turned toward the newly arrived Brachas. "My name is Caleb. I figured I should volunteer before I was volunteered. I studied in England. My English is voted best in the room."

Rebekah waved a hand in denial. "Not with native speakers present."

He smiled and held a playful finger to his lips in her direction. "Shhh."

Turning back to Ma'ayan and Eitan, he continued. "So, we know why you are here, and we are here to help you help us. You want to know about the Overcomers, especially the ones here in the Holy Land. I will start with my namesake, since that is a good way to begin. I am named for Caleb of the Bible. When the Israelites escaped from Egypt, they wandered in disobedience—otherwise known as the desert—for forty years. Because of their disbelief and disobedience, that first generation wasn't allowed into the Promised Land—with the exception of Joshua and Caleb. These two believed God's promise. When they came back from spying in the Promised Land, Caleb said, "We should by all means go up and take possession of it, for we will surely overcome it.

"The Hebrew word for 'overcome' is yachal spelled yud-kaf-lamed—Eitan, you will learn the Hebrew aleph-bet. In English, yachal is translated 'to be able.' Even better, it is 'to exercise power in order to be able.' To overcome is to walk in power. To walk in power, you must first know your power."

"And then there is the word yahal—spelled yud-hay-lamed. This word is 'hope,' an expectant hope in something yet to come. So you see, the Overcomers walk in power and hope."

Ma'ayan looked up from her notes, an idea beginning to form about the shape of the article she would write. She lifted her pen to ask a question. At that moment, the wail of a missile siren ripped through the house.

Chapter Eighteen

A desert wadi near the Dead Sea, Israel

FATHER DA'UD STEPPED out of his cave. Looking up through the narrow wadi walls of rock to the starry sky, he said, "It is not yet time. Remember, the misguided of my people still await, just like the misguided of yours."

No one visible was there to reply.

Father Da'ud had been talking to invisible things for most of his eighty years. Fifty of those years, he had spent here, where there wasn't anyone around to think him crazy—just the few followers who came to be blessed and who brought him food. If they didn't come, Father Da'ud ran out of bread and dates. Then, he simply fasted. He could fast for weeks. The best visions came on an empty stomach, anyway.

The stars were still there, silent and distant. Father Da'ud chuckled, his navel-length beard lifting from his chest as he bent back to look up. "I know You haven't forgotten. I just like to remind You anyway."

He began his methodical walk down the south side of the wadi. He knew this deep canyon as well in the darkness as he did in the daylight. With each step, he spoke another syllable of his prayers blended with Scriptures.

"He will gather you from the nations, O Israel. He will put His spirit on you, and you will know that He is God. Prepare yourself! You will be called to arms. God will make His name holy among you. The nations will know He is with you. He will display His glory among nations."

Father Da'ud continued his walk, quoting scriptures in Arabic and Hebrew and sometimes speaking a language no linguist could classify. Sometimes he stopped on a spot of earth to wrestle with some unmoving issue and only continued walking when he felt it shift in the spirit.

The darkness of night deepened, the shadows grew thicker, and the old prophet kept up his walking intercession.

On his sixth return lap along the north wall, Father Da'ud stopped. Shaking his finger at the sky, he said, "No. That missile will not strike. In the name of the Holy One."

Father Da'ud knew God was listening. He had been listening to the hermit's family since the Messiah had come over two thousand years ago.

TEL AVIV, ISRAEL

Ma'ayan was four, in the attic pretending she was a polar bear. She had seen a picture of a place with white everywhere. Cold-looking white with white bears. Safta Liya told her the polar bears lived far north, and she pointed up at the ceiling. Ma'ayan assumed this meant the attic, since that was the farthest she could go.

When Safta went back to the kitchen, Ma'ayan decided to visit the polar bears. She would pretend she was a polar bear before she got there so that the other bears would be friendly. She crawled up the stairs to the second floor, across the study, and to the little door that led to the attic. She climbed up the narrow stairs, carefully pausing at the top to look around. Where were the bears? She crawled around boxes and under an old table. She moved a stack of photo albums and decided the bears must be sleeping. That seemed like a good idea.

The noise woke her. It was the noise of fear—like a whole city crying. Ma'ayan wanted her mother, but father had told her she was gone.

She called for her anyway, "Mom!"

Only it wasn't Ma'ayan calling out to her mother, it was Eitan calling her above the space-filling sound of the missile siren.

Ma'ayan shook her head, returning to her current self and the room full of people moving toward the door that went not upstairs but downstairs. She grabbed her son's hand.

Shafiq was at her elbow, "Come."

Shafiq led them to the door at the base of the stairs.

Eitan looked at his mother, "Bomb shelter?"

"Yes. Don't worry. It ends soon."

Liya stayed at the end of the line, herding her guests gently toward the shelter: Caleb, Jason, Rebekah, two men Ma'ayan had already forgotten the names of, a couple who had arrived late, and another woman.

At the bottom of the stairs, they passed through a thick door into a cement room with chairs. Liya's bomb shelter had a few more amenities than most. She kept fake flowers in vases and had taped scriptures all along the walls. Boxes of matches and candles lined the floors.

The Overcomers started forming a circle. Liya pulled Ma'ayan and Eitan into it and began speaking in Hebrew. Actually, it wasn't Hebrew. Ma'ayan was so tired and jet lagged she wondered if her mother language had just slipped out of her head. But no, Liya was making sounds. So were the others.

The cement walls began to fill with an undulating, multi-toned kind of song that drowned out the distant siren.

Ma'ayan's muddled exhaustion shifted into clarity. As it had at Della's during Peter's wake, peace entered the room as tangibly as if a person had.

All of a sudden the singing stopped. In the silence, the group realized the siren had stopped, too.

Chapter Nineteen

SUNLIGHT SCATTERED THROUGH the leaves of the olive tree. Ma'ayan blinked in the direction of the window. She had slept through the night.

I am home.

Was home this house? This country? Maybe some of both. But Ma'ayan had the feeling home was something no map could show.

She sat up in bed, looking around at her father's old room. He had grown up in this room, an only child. He had moved back here with four-year-old Ma'ayan and new-born Amit after the death of his young wife in childbirth.

Liya had been the girls' mother and grandmother. She was strong enough to be several generations all in one body. Ma'ayan was in school before she realized other children's mothers weren't also their grandmothers.

Ma'ayan had always loved this room. It had its own doors out into the front garden and high ceilings with an upper bank of windows. It was always filled with light.

The room she had shared with her sister was adjacent. Eitan had slept there. She rose and pulled on a light cotton robe. He wasn't in bed, but he had straightened the covers. Ma'ayan smiled.

She heard voices and continued down the hall and through the foyer. In the kitchen, Liya was at the stove while Eitan sat at the table with a woman who looked like a safta, too. She was speaking to Liya but broke off when she saw Ma'ayan.

Liya turned from the stove. In Hebrew she said, "Aha. She rises before noon. Coffee?"

Ma'ayan kissed her grandmother on the head and said, "Absolutely." She turned toward her son, "See? The Jewish guilt starts already!"

Liya shrugged her shoulders and poured her granddaughter a cup from the small bronze pot on the stove. "Eh, I used most of it on your father. You're lucky."

Ma'ayan accepted the coffee, took a sip, and closed her eyes in pleasure. It was the thick, Turkish coffee Liya had continued to send to her son for years after he and the girls moved to the States. Liya added cardamom, Bedouin-style.

Ma'ayan gave her grandmother another kiss, this time on the cheek. "Heaven. Except for the constant threats of death here, it's heaven."

Liya turned off the stove with one hand while waving the other in the air. "The constant threats of death are not good, no. But they remind us to enjoy what we have while we have it."

She steered Ma'ayan toward the table. "And this morning we have bagels and lachs and soft cheese."

Eitan pulled out a chair for his mom.

Liya pointed to the woman across from her. Shifting to English, she said, "I wait to introduce you until you have your first sip of coffee. This is Mrs. Uziel, a very good friend. She comes each week for breakfast. I missed her last time. She just broke Shiva."

Ma'ayan extended her hand across a plate of pink lachs. "Hello, Mrs. Uziel. Your husband was the professor?"

"Yes."

Eitan looked up from his bagel, "Shiva is the mourning period, right?"

Liya looked at her American great-grandson. "Yes. It is good you know this."

Eitan nodded. "Mom and grandpa taught me some of the traditions." To Mrs. Uziel he said, "I'm sorry. I hope that the people who killed your husband will be caught. Even more, that the rest of them will stop killing."

Ma'ayan tried to not look like a proud mother, but she couldn't help it. She knew her son was a genius, and she loved it when others saw his intelligence. But even more, she loved that Eitan had wisdom. Her son could see beyond the single issue of a murder and its consequences to a broader death that needed to be exchanged for life. In that moment at her grandmother's kitchen table, Ma'ayan felt her hope and purpose were restored. She found herself hoping her writing could—even in the tiniest way—help this group of Overcomers. If it could help them, it would maybe help expose the people who had killed Nikki, Professor Uziel, Peter. And that would be a step toward ending some of the violence. Ma'ayan was beginning to understand that her small ability to assist was sourced in learning what it was to be an Overcomer.

Liya and Mrs. Uziel pushed the plate of bagels and cheese toward Ma'ayan, who began spreading the soft cheese on a bagel half. "Sometimes I forget how much comfort good food can bring."

Mrs. Uziel nodded. "That is understood in the Shiva tradition. Our bodies must continue, even when our spirits might not want to."

Eitan leaned forward. "I started learning more about Jewish traditions—the Hebrew language, too." He pulled out his tablet. "I'll show you something."

Ma'ayan said, "He's a wizard with computers. He has an ongoing birthday and Christmas wish list filled with technology. He preferred this stuff to a car."

Eitan was scrolling through files. "I got an anti-glare cover, finally."

Liya shook her head and Mrs. Uziel smiled.

"See?" Eitan turned the tablet so that the rest of the table could see it, "I downloaded some interactive Hebrew lessons. And this," he pointed to a green link, "this is the funniest. It's the 'Menorapp.'"

Eitan clicked an icon and a digital Menorah began flickering. Liya slapped the table with laughter. "So I don't have to worry about leaving the candle burning on Shabbat, eh?"

Mrs. Uziel was shaking her head. "You should visit the university. I think you would enjoy it. My grandson studies in the computer sciences department. Would you be interested in visiting with him?"

"Absolutely!" Eitan started asking a barrage of questions about when and where.

Ma'ayan turned to Liya, "Is there any further news about the missile attack?"

Liya rose and walked to the flat screen television in the living room. Ma'ayan followed with her coffee and bagel.

Liya handed Ma'ayan the remote control, explaining what was cable and what was DVD before returning to the kitchen.

Ma'ayan found a spot on the couch. The TV was on the same channel they had all watched last night after the siren stopped. This morning, the newscaster was talking about the new Havilah Gas Field, which had successfully begun drilling the day before. The news camera zoomed in and around the floating facility, explaining the drilling procedure and then cutting to the celebration. The workers tossed their hardhats into the air and promptly caught them and put them back on.

A man who looked in charge spoke with unrestrained joy into the microphone, his graying hair lifting in the wind. "At last our dream is being realized: to help provide Israel with her own natural resources. Not only will this discovery of gas greatly increase Israel's GDP, but it is also cheaper and more efficient than oil. This is a moment of great happiness for us all."

The reporter signed off from the gas field, and the anchor segued by saying, "Such celebrations could have been short lived."

The television screen filled with images of the previous evening's missile strike. Captured by video in the dark sky was the flare of a missile being destroyed by the Iron Dome's antimissile. The anchor continued, "Two attacks originated from the Gaza Strip, one aimed at Tel Aviv, but the other aimed at the sea. Authorities believe that Havilah Gas Field was the target. A new Islamic terrorist group has claimed responsibility."

A stiff-looking military analyst appeared next to the anchor, who began asking him questions about the group called the Takbir. "What is the link between the two missile targets?"

The military analyst answered, "The missile attack on Tel Aviv was likely a diversion. It is probable that the enemy hoped our focus would be on averting the attack to a densely populated metropolis instead of the Sea. But we have been prepared for an attack on the gas field. We weren't surprised."

Ma'ayan laughed. To the man on the screen, she said, "You'd never admit you were."

As the news broke off for an electronics commercial, Ma'ayan sipped her coffee, the reporter in her already assimilating information. It was time to find her notebook.

Chapter Twenty

Ariel, Israel

THE MORNING SUNLIGHT filled Azzam's office. Jalil shaded his eyes, wondering why his leader wasn't more upset. "Sir, what do we do? The missile to the gas field was stopped."

Azzam turned from the window. "I am aware of Israel's Iron Dome technology. It would have been a bonus if the missiles—either of them—had reached their targets. Our people in Gaza are…" He shrugged. "Meanwhile, we keep moving forward with the virus until we do something far bigger than launching missiles."

Jalil scratched his beard. "There is another thing, sir."

Azzam looked back up from the papers on his desk.

"The OTF knows about us."

"Did you make contact with our infiltrator?"

"Yes. He learned that one of the OTF had figured out our identity. Our name."

"Don't look so worried, Jalil. That is part of our broader timing. I have Takbir members planted for reasons, like our Mr. Karim. Is he here?"

"Yes, sir. He's speaking with Shakham. He will be here–"

There was a knock at the door. Azzam nodded to Jalil to open it. Shafiq Karim stepped into the Takbir headquarters.

A DESERT WADI NEAR THE DEAD SEA, ISRAEL

Father Da'ud thanked the young man who presented him with a basket of fresh fruit and bread. The morning sun filled the wadi and illuminated the pomegranates.

Their deliverer inclined his head, "Bless you, my father." And with that, the young Abdul-Halim bounded down the valley, back to the jeep that waited out of sight in the next accessible canyon.

Father Da'ud set down the basket and sat beside it. Laying his hands across his next meals, he blessed the food and the hands of those who had brought it. He reached for the knife strapped to his robe's belt and cut open one of the pomegranates. The translucent, ruby seeds gushed open, and their juice ran like blood down the old prophet's weathered hands. He began to eat, slowly, taking just what he needed.

He had finished chewing a piece of bread when Abdul-Halim came back. Father Da'ud looked up, squinting. No. It was someone else.

"Who goes there?" he asked of the man.

The man stepped closer, and Father Da'ud could see he wore the white stone.

The visitor said, "I am a sent one. I have come with a message. Our enemies plan a terrible destruction."

"Yes. They always do."

"Keep praying. Your prayers change things."

Father Da'ud smiled. "Of course. I have already been praying for an unnamed threat. I saw it in my dream last night; it was a different kind of destruction than the missile. I did four prayer walks down the wadi this morning with scriptures from Isaiah. Jerusalem shall be established and will be the praise of the earth."

The visitor bowed, "Thank you. As the B'rit Hadashah says, if two of us agree on Earth, it will be done."

Father Da'ud nodded and noticed his basket of fruit. He picked up a pomegranate, "Would you like one?"

But when he looked past the red fruit in his fist, the sent one was gone. Father Da'ud scratched his mustache, finding a piece of bread still hanging there. If that had been a vision, it had nothing to do with fasting.

FORT WORTH, TEXAS

Della's purple hydrangeas came to her chin. She loved those flowers. She knew they grew so high because she did her walks of prayers and blessings along them. It wasn't just carbon dioxide the plants liked; it was the spirit of power—better than any Miracle-Gro. Or maybe it was the original miracle grow! She chuckled. Try convincing the folks down at the nursery that prayers were the reason her flowers won best of show each year.

Della pulled an ill leaf off a hydrangea stalk and almost jumped. On the other side of the flower stood a man.

Her heart calmed. He wore a white stone, though he wasn't one of the Overcomers she knew.

"What can I do for you?" She asked.

He said, "She arrived safely."

"Oh, good. I saw the news this mornin'. Somethin' always seems to be exploding in Israel, or about to."

The man nodded. "And there are plans for worse. Gather your team. We need intercession."

"Will do. I made a double batch of sweet tea."

Della bent to pick up her gardening basket. "Would you like to come in for a glass?"

But when she looked through her hydrangeas, the stranger was gone.

Chapter Twenty-one
Tel Aviv, Israel

HER FIRST INTERVIEW was about to begin. Ma'ayan had gathered the names and numbers of each of the Overcomers she'd met the night before. It was a short list, but there were more, she was assured. Liya explained, "We meet in small groups in homes. Kind of like the early Church."

Mrs. Uziel hadn't been on the list, but she'd been at breakfast, and Ma'ayan knew to seize an opportunity. The two women sat in Liya's back garden on contoured wooden chairs beneath a lemon tree. Ma'ayan rested her notebook on her crossed knee.

Eitan joined them with his laptop, "I can start my observation of the Great Journalist in action." He made a mock bow toward Ma'ayan and sat at the outdoor table.

Ma'ayan ignored the bow and turned to Mrs. Uziel. "Do you mind if we speak English for Eitan?"

"Not at all. I enjoy the opportunity to use my English."

"Thank you. And thank you for taking the time to do this. Your husband, Leo Uziel—what was he working on before he died?"

"Leo's degree would translate to 'The Science of the Spirit.' I don't think you have such a degree in English-speaking countries. It includes literature, Bible, and history. He was working on a book about the Hebrew aleph-bet: the alphabet. He loved the meanings of the letters and realized how few of his own people understood them. He was working on a book for his students that he hoped to publish one day for everyone.

"Shafiq told me he found a piece of newspaper in Leo's hand after the...explosion." Mrs. Uziel paused and looked down at her own hands. "He had circled the letter vav. After Shafiq and Jason left that day, I went through my husband's papers on that letter. Vav means connection—on many levels.

"In all of the thousands of letters that make up the Torah, the vav is the letter that comes in the exact middle. It is the creative connection between all letters. What is the shape of the vav?"

Ma'ayan looked up from her notebook where she had already sketched the Hebrew letter. "Kind of like a hook."

Mrs. Uziel nodded. "It is the divine hook that connects heaven and earth. It is also the shape of a nail. Nails connect one thing to another. Leo's notes are full of many things. Some he planned to publish, some not. He had friends in the physics department of the university. He loved to talk about quantum things and often joked he was a quantum physicist, too. He told his colleagues that the field they studied was the spirit dimension—the one we cannot see only because we haven't learned to open the eyes of our spirits. We often had professors in our home talking and arguing late into the night. Leo had written that the vav represented the greater reality of heaven connected to the lesser reality of earth. Because of that connection, we can experience the greater reality here and now."

Mrs. Uziel looked at Eitan, "You know the idea of déjà vu?"

Eitan looked up, "Those times you think something has already happened. Like you relive an experience."

"Yes. Some people say that means you are right where

you're supposed to be. Leo said it meant you've slipped into the future and brought it back into the present."

Eitan furrowed his brow. "Like time travel?"

Mrs. Uziel smiled, "That is one way to understand it."

Eitan nodded. "I think I'm going to like learning this language."

Havilah Gas Field

The pipelines were working. The workers were happy. Zadok was happy. He had spent the whole morning just walking the drilling platform, triple checking pipes, people, paperwork.

Yesterday's news footage had made Zadok's dream even more visible to the world. That could be good, and that could be bad. Israel's neighbors could either decide to benefit from the gas harvest by consuming it, or they could decide to be annoyed that it wasn't theirs and try to interfere with the production process—like that new terrorist group had already attempted.

Anything was possible. Today, Zadok decided to focus on the positive possibilities, not the negative ones.

Though the first hurdle was done, there would be more to come. Standing at the railing, looking across the sea in the direction of Israel, Zadok said aloud to his homeland, "We will overcome. We were created to overcome."

He stood there in what looked like silence for over a quarter of an hour. Workers who happened to notice the boss probably thought he was planning a tropical vacation now that his investment was about to pay off. But Zadok was already forming an idea for investing his returns back into his country. As ideas started forming themselves, he turned inside to type them up.

Back in his office, Zadok closed the door and sat back in his desk chair, watching the pictures of his family slide across his computer screen. A digital photo of his son and grand-twins floated by. Zadok hoped to leave behind this legacy for them and the generations he would never see. He touched his mouse, and a blank document appeared. He began typing.

Chapter Twenty-two

Old Jaffa, Israel

THE DAY WAS heating up, but the sun had already passed over the narrow streets, leaving them in warm shade. Ma'ayan remembered running along these ancient stone steps as a girl.

Eitan had his smart phone out taking pictures of everything: the Jaffa blue shutters of windows high in sandstone walls, the low doors leading directly off the street. He stopped in front of one of these doors with an unintelligible date carved above it and asked, "How old is this place?"

"Sections of the old town are almost five thousand years old. According to legend, Jaffa was named after one of Noah's sons, who supposedly built it after the Great Flood. But what I remember most was that the majority of Palestine's newspapers and books were printed here."

"Palestine is the old word for Israel, right?"

"Good memory. Come on, we'll see more later. We'll be late."

They descended the stone street, passed under an archway, and eventually emerged onto the promenade lining the port. The western sun lit everything to a hot brightness.

Caleb was sitting at the outer row of outdoor tables fronting one of many cafes. Awnings snapped in the breeze, and the scent of fish from the bobbing boats along the promenade blended with freshly ground espresso.

Caleb rose to greet them. "I thought you might like to meet somewhere Eitan could explore."

Eitan shook Caleb's hand. "Thanks. I've never seen buildings older than the nineteenth century."

Ma'ayan also shook Caleb's hand and then looked at her son, "Sorry about that. Working moms don't seem to travel much."

As they sat down, Eitan shrugged. "Hey, I appreciate it more now."

Caleb laughed. "He doesn't sound like the American teenagers I've met."

Ma'ayan scanned the caffeine options, wondering what would help her stay awake until dark. She set the menu down and looked at her son. "You know, I sometimes wonder if he's even human. I keep waiting for the fatal flaw to emerge, but at almost eighteen, he's kind of perfect."

"Mom."

After the waitress came and took their orders, Caleb clapped his hands. "So. What do you want to know?"

Ma'ayan pulled out her notebook. "My son is shadowing me for a journalism class. Do you mind if he asks questions, too?"

"Of course not."

"Eitan, you want to start?"

He leaned forward, "How can you tell something is going to happen?"

Caleb smiled. "Good question. Hmm. I will try to answer that by describing prophecy."

Ma'ayan asked, "Are the Overcomers prophets?"

"Some of us. There are different kinds of prophecy. We believe that everyone has the ability to prophesy, but not everyone is a prophet by calling."

Ma'ayan continued, "And you believe there are still prophets today?"

"Of course. Here is a story you will like because you are a journalist. You have likely heard of Theodor Herzl. He was a Jewish journalist from Vienna. He was in Paris reporting on the trial of Alfred Dreyfus in the late nineteenth century. Dreyfus was accused of espionage, and the crowd started chanting "Kill the traitor!" But soon, that chant changed to, 'Kill the Jew!'

"Herzel was shaken by the contempt for his people. Two years later, he convened the first World Zionist Congress in 1879. The congress selected the flag and anthem for Israel: a flag in the blue and white of the prayer shawl. And the anthem Hatikvah, 'The Hope.'

"Herzl prophesied a State of Israel within fifty years. Fifty years later, in 1947, the United Nations voted Israel into existence. The prophecy of Isaiah 66:8 had come true: a nation was born in a day."

Ma'ayan set her coffee down. She didn't know if it was the return to her homeland, these Overcomers, or a combination of both, but she kept experiencing strange splits in time. She wasn't entirely sure what a quantum moment was, but she was beginning to think that's what she was having.

Eitan was typing notes onto his tablet, forgetting to ask questions.

Ma'ayan looked at Caleb. "So a flag and a song helped bring about a country?"

"Perhaps that's one way to say it. You could also say that a man walked in his power to see the destiny of a nation and called it into being."

Eitan tilted his head as a seagull soared by. "You can do that?"

Caleb looked at him. "You can do that."

"How?"

Taking the last sip of his coffee, Caleb looked out to the fishing boats. "I have another contact for you both."

HAARATZ NEWSPAPER HEADQUARTERS, TEL AVIV, ISRAEL

Shoken Street was busy as always. Ruben looked out his office window, turning his gaze to a palm tree. It would be a great day to be at the beach. He couldn't remember the last time he and Margie had taken a picnic and spent the day by the water.

The phone rang.

"Yes?"

His secretary told him, "Your visitors are here. Would you like me to send them up?"

"Please. And can you tell Margie to join me? Thank you."

Margie called next. "For what?"

"American visitors. Maybe something you want to cover—fellow yanks in the Holy Land."

"We don't really use 'yanks' any more. But for new windows, I'll be a 'yank' and cover whatever you want, darling."

Ruben couldn't help but smile. That woman drove him crazy. And he loved it. Loved her. He still saw her as the young, American college grad she'd been when they met at the kibbutz. She had offered him a tomato from the basket she held with both hands. He could still taste that tomato.

Margie was still talking, "Ruben. Ruben?"

"Right. Come over."

He hung up, and moments later his wife entered, followed by a teenage boy and a woman perhaps a decade younger than Margie.

Ruben extended his hand, "Caleb told me you'd be coming. Ma'ayan? I'm Ruben, and this is my wife, Margie. Margie works for our English edition, and I am an editor for our Hebrew paper."

Ma'ayan smiled, shook hands with both of them, and

introduced Eitan as her shadow journalist. The shadow journalist was trying not to yawn.

Ruben had an idea. "Since I don't have much time, let's divide forces. Margie, would you like to give Eitan a tour of the headquarters? Ma'ayan, you can interview me. You'll have more information between you that way."

Margie smiled at her smart husband, Eitan looked relieved, and Ma'ayan nodded.

Margie put her hand on Eitan's shoulder. "Onward to the secrets of the publishing industry."

When the door closed, Ruben offered Ma'ayan a chair, and she tilted her head. "So what don't you want my son to know?"

In Hebrew, Ruben said, "That I could see he was about to fall asleep."

Ma'ayan tried her mother tongue. It felt rusty. "I feel the same. Do you mind if I stand?"

"Not at all."

Ruben looked above his glasses out onto Shoken Street. Another group appeared to be gathering with banners. He pointed. "In this country, you can always count on someone being angry with you."

Ma'ayan joined him at the window, watching a few young men holding a banner protesting a recent article published by the Haaretz.

She looked at the editor, his face deeply lined with years of words and worry. "What made you become an Overcomer?"

He smiled, changing the direction of those lines. "Like you, I already was one. I just didn't know it."

"Why don't you wear the necklace?"

"Originally, only the Overcomers themselves knew what the stones meant. But when the proverbial signs and wonders started happening—healings, accurate predictions, and so on—government agencies started noticing that the people responsible were wearing the stones."

He paused before resuming, an unspoken thought crossing beneath his reading glasses. "I think we will be known by the public soon, too. For that reason, I don't wear the necklace. I must be the thinking sheep in wolves' clothing; otherwise, I won't be able to do my job here. And I am needed here. When we can see what's coming, we can decide what to emphasize in print and online."

He paused, looking out again at the young men shaking the banner with force. "You were right. I did want to speak to you without your son present. Be careful. Safety is an illusion anywhere, but especially here. The Overcomers are being watched, so you will be, too. You and your son."

Chapter Twenty-three

ISA, Tel Aviv, Israel

REBEKAH FOUND HERSELF daydreaming about dinner while her computer screen danced with columns of code.

She couldn't put her finger on it, but she had the sense that something somewhere wasn't right. Now that was a nice, tangible report to give Mr. Ben-Ami. Thankfully, he trusted her instincts—they had come in quite useful before.

She checked the news feed on a different computer screen, looking for signs of compromised systems anywhere in the world.

Most targets were completely oblivious their systems were compromised. Rebekah knew for a fact that no computer was immune. Diplomats, journalists, prime ministers, military...she'd seen it all.

She was deciding whether to make schnitzel when she got home when she realized what seemed off; the bandwidth on one of the computers was more sluggish than it had been yesterday.

She closed the applications that normally transferred massive data. The network usage didn't drop.

Aha. She ran a few more checks and was almost relieved to find something happening. She could swing into action now. And the action was to set up a honey pot.

She would try to identify malicious servers by monitoring traffic directed by the infected honey pot—the infected computer. In this way, the Shin Bet could detect malware and see who was responsible for the attacks. That attribution was vital to prevent whatever further damage was planned. And in Israel, damage was always planned.

Rebekah looked up at the Shin Bet motto she kept above her row of computers: "The Unseen Shield."

She sighed. Just another day behind the scenes, trying to help save the world.

Liya's garden was a welcome place to rest, especially since Ma'ayan and Eitan had started back home during Tel Aviv rush hour. Liya no longer drove, but her neighbor's daughter Miriam had graciously lent Ma'ayan her tiny Nissan. It technically had air conditioning, but judging by the sound it made when Eitan tried to turn it on, it had died a while ago.

Mother and son were happy to sit in the shade, sip mint tea, and help Liya polish the silver for the Passover Seder tomorrow. Ma'ayan was trying to forget Ruben's warning, especially since he supposedly saw into the future. She looked at Eitan and wondered what the editor had seen.

Liya held up a knife to the sky, checking for tarnish. "So, Eitan, you have celebrated Passover in America, yes?"

Eitan nodded, scrubbing at a fork. "We usually go to Galveston to Aunt Amit's. Grandpa is there, too."

Liya set down the knife. "Yes, Jeremiah loved the Seder. When he was your age, he would–"

Just then, Miriam bounded into the garden, "Ma Nishma?"

She looked at Eitan, "That means, 'What's up?'"

Eitan gave an embarrassed smile and examined the shining fork he was holding.

Ma'ayan tried not to smile. Hmm, her son was a human teenage boy, after all.

Liya waved Miriam to her side and asked her to help them clear off the silver and set the garden table for dinner.

Miriam started with Eitan's fork and a wink, quickly gathering the remaining silver and whisking it off with the energy of a sixteen-year old.

Ma'ayan was still trying not to smile. She asked Liya, "How often does Miriam come by?"

Liya shrugged. "Every other day during the week. Sometimes more. This week more, with Pesach. She likes getting away from her younger brothers. And I pay her. Like most children, she works at home for free."

Miriam returned with a tray in time to hear Liya. She pouted. "I am not a child." She set down the tray. "See? Children cannot make dinner so fast."

Dinner was a simple one: The rest of last night's hummus, beets, and soft cheese that Miriam had supplemented with some freshly cut cucumbers, tomatoes, and toast. Everyone was hungry, and everyone but Miriam was tired. She stayed to finish the chicken broth for the Matzah soup while Liya simply said she was going to bed, blew a kiss to the garden, and headed to her room.

Ma'ayan's jet lag was bone-deep. She yawned until her tonsils ached and mumbled to Eitan, "Going to bed?"

He tried to look awake as he stretched and stood, "I think I'll watch TV for a few minutes. Night, Mom."

She narrowed her eyes at him as he gave her a quick kiss on the cheek. He never watched TV. Miriam's head popped out the garden door. "Eitan, you help me hold the soup...how do you say? Pan? Bowl?" Her English mysteriously seemed to fade as she looked at Eitan with her beautiful, dark eyes.

Ma'ayan shook her head, both to stay awake long

enough to make it to her room and to show that she was too tired to play chaperone.

She returned her son's kiss on the cheek, adding with a smile, "Just keep all TV and activities rated G."

Chapter Twenty-four
Fort Worth, Texas

Jesse Mae swatted Della on the shoulder with the bright orange petals of a zinnia. "Passover's startin' in Israel about now."

Della turned, unsurprised to see her friend standing in the garden behind her. "Yep. Strange to think the sun is setting somewhere else."

Jesse Mae put her hands on her hips, "Hmm. So much for trying to make you jump. What, could you sense I was here?"

Della grabbed the zinnia and swatted Jesse Mae back. "Nope. I heard you crunchin' on the gravel."

"Well. You gonna offer me tea?"

"You never need invitations, and you know it. In fact, you can pour me a glass. I've been working in this garden all morning. Plus, I pray better with sweet tea."

Jesse Mae laughed and went inside to get the pitcher of tea Della constantly kept in the refrigerator. She filled two tall glasses with ice and tea and brought both out to the porch.

Della was sitting in a faded plastic Adirondack chair, feet propped up on an old citrus crate. She accepted her glass and held it aloft to clink with Jesse Mae's. "Here's to peace and freedom."

"And to fulfillment of prophecy."

TEL AVIV, ISRAEL

It was only the first glass of wine. There were three more to go at a Passover Seder. Ma'ayan looked over her glass toward Liya at the head of the table. Her grandmother wore a white robe, leading the traditional ceremony that Ma'ayan knew so well.

Those seated at the table set down their wine glasses one by one. Ma'ayan's eyes swept around from left to right: Eitan, Liya, Jason, Rebekah, the empty place setting for Elijah, and Shafiq. Jason refilled the glasses.

Everyone washed their hands in the bowls of water near their plates. Ma'ayan was having a hard time concentrating on the ceremony. Something was making her nervous.

Liya started talking about the significance of the Passover plate in front of her. She passed around the parsley. "Dip the parsley in the salt water. At first it will taste sweet. Then it will taste bitter. This represents the Israelites in Egypt. At first their time was sweet; then they became slaves and their time was bitter. In the same way, at first our lives taste sweet, but then sin makes them bitter."

Ma'ayan realized what was making her uncomfortable: Shafiq. The space between them felt charged with electricity—at least from her perspective. He looked intent on his parsley as he chewed it. Ma'ayan found herself wondering if she had any stuck in her teeth. Focus, girl! She told herself.

Next came the first piece of Matzah. Liya broke one of the three pieces of unleavened bread that nestled in a cloth. She returned half of that piece to its place and set aside the other piece for the Afikoman and began telling the Haggadah. Ma'ayan enjoyed hearing "The Story" in Israel. Liya told it mostly in English for Eitan's benefit.

The symbolic meal continued: a piece of the Matzah, the lamb bone, Maror (another bitter herb), the charoset.

Eitan looked at his mother as he finished chewing on the fruit and nut paste meant to symbolize the mortar the Israelites used when making bricks as slaves in Egypt. He'd never eaten that part of the Seder—he couldn't stand the taste. Ma'ayan smiled at him—proud of him for trying.

Liya announced that the meal would be served, and Eitan exhaled.

Rebekah helped serve the Matzah ball soup. Shafiq cut from the leg of lamb. Ma'ayan sent the sweet carrots, roasted potatoes, and salad around the table.

Ma'ayan sipped her wine and wondered what Elijah thought of all the places set for him at tables in Israel this evening. She sent him a silent blessing and realized Shafiq was asking her a question as the others began discussing the tighter Kosher rules of Passover.

Ma'ayan smiled, "I'm sorry, what was that?"

Shafiq repeated, "Why do Messianic Jews still set a place for Elijah? He was to prepare the way for the Messiah. And the Messiah already came."

Had he read her mind? Well, she hadn't been thinking that exact thought, but she had been thinking about Elijah. And who thinks about Elijah?

Ma'ayan poked at her carrots with her fork. "Tradition, I suppose. But since He's supposed to be coming either way—for the first time in the minds of Jews and the second in the minds of Christians—it's still relevant. Religion is a complicated thing."

He nodded. "Religion and spirituality are not synonyms."

Ma'ayan looked at him closely, realizing she could use their conversation as an informal interview. "I agree. I'm an advocate of spirituality. Religion just seems to start arguments and wars."

Shafiq gave a small smile. "May I tell you a story?"

Ma'ayan smiled back. "Of course. You're talking to a journalist. I love stories."

Shafiq's smile expanded. "My father served in top-level government missions. Before I left to begin my military service, he told me this story. He was involved in an operation attempting to thwart the move of terrorists who had kidnapped a prominent religious leader. Intel discovered the location of the hostage, and my father's team traveled to the desert canyons near the Dead Sea.

"After their drop in the dead of night, deep into a wadi crevice, the team stationed themselves not far from the place the hostage was believed to be held. From where he was positioned, my father saw someone walking casually toward him in the darkness. My father aimed his gun at the old man who held up his hand, greeted my father by his name, and introduced himself. 'I am the one sent to give you a solution to the problem you came to solve. It is this: The degree of complexity in your problem will determine the degree of illumination you will receive. Look for the illumination.' And then the man turned and walked away.

"My father had heard of the desert mystics with skepticism. But something about that old man's presence was genuine, even though my father hadn't lowered his gun the entire time the man had been talking. The stranger could have been sent from the enemy, but my father somehow knew he was to be trusted—though he would have a hard time explaining that 'knowledge' to the next in command.

"My father stood there, his gun still raised in the direction the old seer had gone. He heard a faint movement. He turned and saw another figure appear in the dark. This figure approached at an awkward shuffle, hands at sides. Through his scope, my father saw that the figure was dressed as a sniper with a full-face mask. Still, my father couldn't pull the trigger. Something was wrong. The words of the old man coursed through him. Look for the illumination.

"As if on cue, the moon began to rise over the lip of the canyon wall, illuminating two other figures crouching behind the 'sniper.'

"It turns out the man dressed as a sniper was the hostage—the religious leader—his mouth taped beneath the mask and his arms and legs restricted. The terrorists' goal had been for the special ops team to kill the disguised hostage. The terrorists would have then pinned the murder on the government. You can imagine the different directions that could have gone.

"After the hostage was safely returned, my father returned to that wadi and found the old seer. He sat with him for many days, listening and learning. He decided to follow the way the seer followed. It was a way not locked to tradition and manmade rules. It was a Way of the Spirit. He raised me and my brothers to follow it, too."

Ma'ayan had been so engrossed in the story, she had forgotten to taste her soup. She did so now, noticing the depth of flavor in the homemade broth. She made a mental note to compliment Miriam on her cooking and glanced at Eitan. Liya was teaching him Hebrew words: Passover, Pesach. "The Name," Ha Shem.

Rebekah and Jason were whispering and smiling.

Ma'ayan took another sip of wine, thinking that the depth of the man next to her was far greater than that of the soup. She finally said, with a smile and an awareness of its truth, "You are right about the difference between religion and spirituality."

Jason had risen to pass out slices of honey cake, and he

heard this last part. "You too are talking about deep stuff. Here's something sweet to make religion go down easy."

Shafiq laughed, and Ma'ayan realized that was the first time she'd seen him express humor.

Ma'ayan accepted her honey cake with thanks. Though her conversation with Shafiq hadn't turned into a useful interview, it had given her something even more useful: a reminder of forces at work far greater than her own. The realization was a relief. She took a bite of the cake and smiled at many levels of sweetness.

Chapter Twenty-five

Ariel, Israel

SHAHKAM WAS CHUCKLING. He had logged into the Arabs for Israel site and was posting a Happy Passover message. When readers clicked on the link, it would visibly take them to a spinning Star of David, and invisibly it would give him remote access to their computers—access he would use over the next days, along with many other planted viruses. He enjoyed this latent phase—knowing he had control and the users had no idea. He felt like Allah must feel.

He scanned through some of the recent blog entries on the site. How could his own people support the Jews? Infidels! Was he really reading this? He increased the font size and found himself reading that Arabs have been indoctrinated with hate, that jihad against non-Muslims was no way for peace, that love would—

Shahkam heard a sharp intake of breath behind him and turned. Jalil was leaning over his shoulder.

Jalil straightened. "What is this?"

Shahkam, feeling attacked, popped straight up from his chair ready to retaliate. Voice raised, he pointed at his screen, "These traitors! They, too, should suffer as Israel will suffer!"

Jalil realized that if he said anything, the volatile computer prodigy would take it wrong. He simply held up his hands and walked away, those sentences he'd read expanding in his head, in his heart.

Tel Aviv, Israel

The third glass of Seder wine came with the saying of grace, the forth after Hallel—the singing of the Psalms.

Since there were no children around, Liya decided against hiding the Afikoman. Ma'ayan remembered running around with her sister, Amit, trying to find the hidden piece of Matzah, more intent on winning the prize than understanding its symbolism as the sacrificial lamb.

As the Seder ended, everyone leaned back in their chairs in unison.

Rebekah asked, "Ma'ayan, would you and Eitan like to go to the beach tomorrow?"

Eitan roused from sleepiness. "Yes! Mom?"

Ma'ayan was less enthusiastic. She loved the beach, but she didn't love getting into beachwear. She looked at her son, "Eitan, you go. I didn't bring a swimsuit." Actually, she didn't own a swimsuit.

Rebekah waved her hand in the air at this non-existent limitation. "Of course you must go to the beach. I have an idea. I will come early and take you to my favorite shops in the old town. Then we'll get things for lunch at the market. Be'az be sababa: We'll have a picnic.

Eitan said, "That's great." He turned to Ma'ayan. "That will work, right?"

Jason said, "I can't make the market part, but I'll stake out a good spot at the beach. Be sure to bring your phones so we can coordinate. Eitan, you're welcome to join me if you want to skip the shopping. Shafiq, care to join us?"

Shafiq shook his head. "I have work."

Rebekah began clearing the dishes.

Ma'ayan felt immobile. A swimsuit? Tomorrow? As Eitan also rose to help clear the dishes, Shafiq touched Ma'ayan on the shoulder as he had done at the airport. "May I show you something?"

She blinked but followed him as he stood and walked toward the doors that led out into the garden. The night sky was clear, the moon bright. Ma'ayan realized that when she looked up, she could be standing in Texas. But she wasn't. And she wasn't standing alone.

Looking up, Shafiq said, "Would you say the moon is beautiful?"

Surprised, Ma'ayan said, "Of course. It is the moon."

He looked at her. "Even with its craters and scars?"

Ma'ayan felt her face flush and was glad they stood in the dark.

He asked another question, "Would you say you are beautiful?"

Ma'ayan kept her eyes on the moon, saying nothing.

He continued, "Of course. You are Ma'ayan."

Silence rested between them—not a separating silence, but a connecting one. Even though they stood a foot apart, Ma'ayan could feel Shafiq's spirit around her. It was such a tangible feeling that she reached up to touch her shoulder, half expecting something to be there. She touched her own skin.

His words, "you are Ma'ayan," seemed to have a deeper, fuller meaning than just a name people called her. In those words lived something vast and eternal. Without knowing what to call that unknown implication, Ma'ayan acknowledged it, accepted it. Was this part of the power of the Overcomers? Was this what Peter had meant when he said to overcome she must first become?

She felt on the brink of understanding when Eitan called from the kitchen, "Mom, Rebekah and Jason are leaving."

Ma'ayan looked at Shafiq, gave him a small smile, and turned to go inside. Without turning, he said, "The answer is 'yes.'"

Ma'ayan blushed again. Inside, it was warm and smelled like honey cake and coffee. Ma'ayan hoped her blush had faded as she hugged the couple goodbye.

Rebekah clasped her hands, "I'll pick you up at 10:00 tomorrow morning. Good night."

Ma'ayan hoped Shafiq would be going, too, but he sent Liya off to bed and stayed to help Ma'ayan until every last dish was washed. Eitan volunteered to sweep the floor, watching the rough and ready Arab delicately dry the crystal wine glasses and return them to the dining room hutch.

When the kitchen was as clean as it could be, Shafiq turned to mother and son, gave a small bow, and said, "I will leave you now. Rest well."

Ma'ayan and Eitan walked Shafiq to the garden gate.

Shafiq said, "Make sure it is locked behind me. Good night."

"Good night." Ma'ayan watched him walk toward a motorcycle. She squinted through the darkness. Was that...?

"A Triumph, Mom! He rides a Triumph like you." Eitan looked at his mother as if this were some vital fact she should not overlook.

"Indeed. Come on, I'm exhausted. Did you have a good time?"

Eitan nodded, whispering as they returned inside. "I think I'd like to stay here a while."

Ma'ayan looked at him, "What do you mean by 'a while?'"

"Don't worry. I still want to go to college. But I'd like to stay here for the summer—take Hebrew classes."

Ma'ayan gave him a hug. "I'm sure that's a good idea. Just don't make me commit to anything right before bed. Lila tov."

"Lila tov, ma'am."

Ma'ayan returned to her room, tossed on a nightshirt, and climbed into bed. She pulled on the small, corded light mounted to the wall near her pillow. The low wattage barely reached her journal. The moonlight came through the terrace doors and lay across her in rectangles.

She lifted her pen, intending to write down as much as she could remember of her dinner conversation with Shafiq. Ma'ayan looked down at her page, surprised. She had written, "Shafiq gives me hope that my heart has not turned to stone."

The moonlight continued to cover her in quiet light.

Chapter Twenty-six

S HE WAITED IN the Wexler's dining room. The large painting of the owl looked different. It looked different because the owl was no longer in the painting. It had flown out and was perching on the top of a silver Menorah in the middle of the vast table.

Ma'ayan was the only person in the room, but she felt like she was with a friend—not a bird. She turned and walked silently toward the bird's perch. She reached out her arm toward the feathers, noticing the Jaffa blue sleeve of her dress.

The owl said, "Careful. If you touch me, you will learn to fly."

"And why wouldn't I want to fly?"

"Once you can fly, you will see into and over things that you could not see before. Once you have this sight, you will have more responsibility."

"I can handle responsibility."

"Even if it means facing danger to find someone?"

"Who?"

The owl echoed her question back to her, "Who, who, who?"

All of a sudden Ma'ayan wasn't looking at the owl but at a vague darkness. She blinked. It was the ceiling of her bedroom in Tel Aviv. And the sound wasn't the owl calling, it was her phone; she'd just changed her ringtone to a birdcall.

Groggy, she reached for the phone and silenced it. It was three in the morning. The area code was Fort Worth.

She picked up and croaked, "Hello?"

"Oh, shoot. I forgot the time difference. This isn't the middle of the night for you is it?"

Della.

"Yes, but that's fine. What happened?"

"The Mossad agent found Peter's killer."

Ma'ayan could feel her sleeping pulse begin to quicken. "And?"

Della sighed, "He killed himself before they could take him into custody. I'm sorry, hon. No answers there."

Ma'ayan had known Peter so briefly that she wasn't even sure she was mourning. When she thought of him now, she couldn't really feel anything. But she had a hunch the numbness was a cover for an emotion she hadn't given room to express itself.

Della asked, "I also called 'cause I have a word and a prayer for you. Which do you want first?"

Ma'ayan couldn't help but laugh. "How about the order you said them."

"Done. Here's the word: In the natural realm, you know something exists when you see it. In the supernatural, you know something exists when you don't see it."

The owl had talked about seeing. The owl. Ma'ayan shook her head, almost losing her phone in the sheets.

"And here's the prayer: May you have moments this week when your human powers intersect with supernatural powers and nothing is impossible to you. Jesse Mae said you'll need to remember that."

Great.

"Thanks, Della. And thank you for telling me about Peter. I guess it's some closure."

"Hmmph. I know God knows what He's doin', but sometimes I take issue with how He does it. Go back to sleep now. Hugs from Texas. Gotta run."

The signal ended. Ma'ayan pulled on the light cord near her pillow and fumbled through the papers on her nightstand. Where was that paper?

There. She scanned Victor Wexler's letter, finding what she was looking for: Invite revelation in your dreams. Jesse Mae says you'll receive instruction.

Ma'ayan echoed Della's "Hmmph" adding, "Well, the invitation seems to be working. Now if only I can figure out what the revelation means."

She slapped the letter back on top of the pile. As she reached to turn off the light, she found a large, white feather resting on the lampshade.

ARIEL, ISRAEL

Azzam could smell emotions. He knew if one of his men was in love, in financial distress, or in a spiritual crisis.

Jalil was in the latter. As he stood before his boss, waiting for Azzam to say something—anything—Jalil started to sweat.

Azzam turned from the window and crossed to where Jalil stood. Azzam thumped his hand on the man's shoulder. Jalil flinched.

So it was. Azzam would just have to give the man a chance to prove his devotion to the Takbir, to Allah. But first, Azzam couldn't resist a bit of education for this wavering follower.

"Jalil, most of our job has already been accomplished. So many people walk through their lives with no vision. They live in a state of routine survival. That is the perfect state for us to gain power. Only once the façade of infrastructure is torn down can the truer instability be visible. Then we can rise up and demand allegiance to Allah. Allah or death."

With his last words, Azzam looked Jalil straight in the eye, waiting.

When Jalil finally blinked, Azzam said, "I have an assignment for you. Someone is compromising the development of our computer virus. This person needs to be removed."

Jalil's pupils dilated and then contracted so quickly, a less observant man would not have noticed. Azzam was nothing if not observant. He pulled his hand away.

Jalil nodded and cast his eyes toward the floor, as if feeling Azzam's knowing. "Yes, sir."

Azzam turned back to the window, wishing he could see his homeland. Iran was invisible through the glass but quite visible in his heart, in his every action. He would bring supremacy to his country. They had waited long enough.

Jalil cleared his throat, "Sir?"

Azzam didn't bother turning. "Fakhir will tell you the details. He is waiting in the courtyard."

Jalil nodded. "Inshallah."

At this, Azzam did turn. "Allah does go with me. I hope he goes with you, too, my friend."

Chapter Twenty-seven
Old Jaffa, Israel

O
LD JAFFA'S SKYLINE of mosques, churches, syn-
agogues, and palm trees lay against a backdrop
of Mediterranean blue skies. It was late morning,
and the breeze moved, cool, through the streets. Rebekah
led Ma'ayan into a warren of pedestrian lanes, bursting
with boutiques and galleries.

Rebekah had been narrating ever since they paid for
parking near the promenade. "The north port of Tel Aviv
is known for its shopping. But I always prefer Yafo, the
Old Jaffa. It's so romantic here."

She stopped in front of a jewelry store with a sigh,
tucking her red hair behind her ears. "This is my dream
store. See that ring? It's the one I want for my engagement."

Ma'ayan was happy to postpone swimsuit shopping as
long as possible. She leaned close to the glass to admire
the swirling filigree of gold nestling an emerald at its
center. She watched Rebekah's dreamy expression. "Are
you expecting Jason to propose, soon?"

Rebekah nodded. "We've talked about it. I think he
wants his parents to meet me first, which I understand."

Ma'ayan said, "The Wexlers are good people. I'm sure
they would embrace you as family."

Rebekah turned from the display to look at Ma'ayan.
"Thank you. Come, we're here for you, not me."

She led Ma'ayan a bit farther and stopped in front of a
timeworn door with just an artistic set of wrought-iron

numbers above it. The windows, far larger than the small door, looked into a spacious and inviting boutique of women's clothing.

Rebekah opened the door and entered. Ma'ayan stepped onto the thick threshold of stone and just stood there. She hadn't been shopping in years. In fact, the outfit she wore—old khakis and a t-shirt—may well have been around when Eitan's father was. She felt the familiar dread of entering a place where women knew how to dress themselves and enjoyed doing so.

Rebekah turned, saw Ma'ayan rooted to the doorway, and smiled. She led her over to a petite woman in diaphanous folds of soft earth tones and bright red glasses who shook Ma'ayan's hand warmly and avoided looking overtly at her faded khakis.

In Hebrew, the woman introduced herself as Sigalit. "Welcome to my store. What are you looking for?"

Ma'ayan wanted to say, "The back exit," but restrained herself. She couldn't seem to think of anything to say—in English or in Hebrew. What was she looking for? Sigalit wasn't selling answers to life's questions, but she was selling some admittedly gorgeous clothing.

Rebekah spoke in Hebrew, "She needs a swimsuit."

Sigalit nodded. "Let's start with a dress you can wear over the suit."

She led Ma'ayan to a whitewashed wall with tension-wire lighting crisscrossing above a suspended rod that held a line of dresses. The rod swayed gently when Sigalit touched one of the blue dresses. She pulled it and an ivory dress in a bias cut from the rod, handing them to Ma'ayan and guiding her to the dressing room.

"I will bring you some suits. Start with these."

Ma'ayan felt like she was breaking some unwritten pact she'd made for herself without realizing it. She hung the dresses near a mirror—a full-length mirror, no less, and hesitated. She vaguely remembered the feeling of disappointment once upon her last shopping excursion.

But then she remembered how Shafiq had talked about the moon.

She took a deep breath, removed her t-shirt and khakis, and tried on the ivory dress. She didn't look in the mirror until she had it on. When she looked, she was shocked. She liked it. It liked her.

Ma'ayan hadn't looked in a full-length mirror in years. She'd taken the one off her closet door back home to avoid catching sight of herself in it. But this dress... If there were smart phones, there were smart dresses. It covered some things and revealed others.

"Ma'ayan? How is it?"

A smile spread across Ma'ayan's face, and her voice reflected it, "Better than expected. Much better than expected."

•ק•

Two shopping bags later, Ma'ayan had not just one, but two swimsuits, two dresses, a new pair of pants, a skirt, several shirts, and a cardigan. They all intermixed.

"Even this black swimsuit you can wear for the evening with the skirt," advised Sigalit, who had chosen everything for Ma'ayan in addition to giving her advice for a hairstyle to complement her jawline and the name of a stylist to create it.

Ma'ayan's head was swirling as she and Rebekah headed toward the Port's food market for picnic items.

Rebekah gave Ma'ayan a quick hug. "You will not regret those things."

Ma'ayan laughed, "My wallet might."

Rebekah gave her a knowing smile, "Sometimes, a woman must invest in herself before a man does."

Ma'ayan was surprised at this and started to ask what Rebekah meant, but the young woman had entered a large, covered market packed with every kind of food and every smell of food. Ma'ayan's thoughts went immediately from men to bread as she found herself face-to-pastry with a mound of bourekas, small breads filled with sheep cheese.

Rebekah pulled her cloth market bags from her purse and began to fill them. Bourekas, knafneh—a Palestinian pastry soaked in Rose water syrup. Hummus dripping with olive oil, olives stuffed with garlic. Pita, tabouleh, tomatoes. Pomegranates, figs, halvah.

The market bags began to get heavy, and the women's stomachs reminded them they were empty. Rebekah hefted a bag in the direction of a small Arab café along the outer wall and said, "Let's get something here before we go."

She ordered two of the kefir-like yogurt drinks for which Ma'ayan insisted on paying. They sat in the tiny, yellow plastic chairs and sipped on the drinks.

Rebekah took a deep drink and set down her glass. "Here is where the Arabs and Jews know how to come together: over food. That's another reason why I like to come to Yafo. It seems these markets, more than anywhere, are a model for Israel. For living in harmony."

Ma'ayan pulled out her notebook. "Great point. Sorry— give me a second to scrawl an idea."

While writing, she looked up for a second at the jovial and rotund Arab man who had served them their drinks. He was a businessman with a family, just like the Jewish man who had sold them their pomegranates. She hoped someday the extremists from both nations—with all their historical baggage—could exist so symbiotically.

Ma'ayan closed her notebook and finished her yogurt. "Like you, I think for a living."

Rebekah took a last sip, methodically arranged and re-arranged the items on the table, and said, "Yes. Even now, I can't stop thinking about work."

She motioned to the man who had served them. He said, "one minute."

Rebekah smiled and continued her earlier thought. "Just before Passover, I found something strange. I'll probably head back to the office tonight and see if anything has changed. But I'm trying not to think about work when I'm away. So let's get to the beach and eat all of this food!"

When Ma'ayan stood to clear their glasses, Rebekah started to stand, too. But she heard something with her spirit and remained seated. Time slowed. In Rebekah's peripheral vision, she could see Ma'ayan holding the glasses toward the counter and the man reaching for them. They seemed frozen in the uncompleted exchange.

Rebekah focused on her spirit as a voice entered it, saying: "You have an appointment for a larger mission in a different place than you could have ever anticipated. You will receive and share a word." And with that, time resumed, the glasses exchanged, and Rebekah stood to go.

The two women left the colorful and noisy hustle of the market, Ma'ayan thinking of her article and Rebekah of what she had just heard. The car-lined promenade was thick with pedestrians and vehicles during lunch hour. As they neared Rebekah's Hyundai, she warned, "Watch for cars when you get in."

Ma'ayan went around to the back of the car to put her clothing purchases in the trunk. A van approached quite fast and close—Rebekah wasn't kidding. The trunk made a strange sound as Ma'ayan closed it.

It wasn't the trunk. When Ma'ayan looked up, she saw

just Rebekah's legs being dragged into the open side door of the van. It had stopped right against the small car.

Rebekah yelled out, "The spine!" just as the van door closed. The vehicle was already darting away before Ma'ayan had a chance to react. She ran forward toward Rebekah's driver door. It was still gaping open, market bags on the pavement, car keys sinking into the fallen open hummus.

Chapter Twenty-eight
Fort Worth, Texas

Victor Wexler leaned back in his chair. "As the Prime Minister said, maybe the Muslim extremists don't hate the West because of Israel; they hate Israel because of the West. The West has to wake up. We're already at war. We don't need a draft and rations to tell us that. And now, we think Russia and Islamic forces are concocting something. Probably have been for quite a while."

Asher, the Mossad agent, set down his coffee cup without a sound on the saucer. "More than you know. Yes, we have confirmation that Russia and Iran have joined forces."

Victor narrowed his eyes. He waited for Asher to continue.

"We're dealing with two different ideologies that come together to make a deadly partnership. Russia's short-term interests fuel Iran's long-term interests of destruction. Generally, Russians aren't letting the afterlife define their political strategy, whereas the Islamic eschatology adopted by terrorist Iranians is a very afterlife-driven one. Russian leaders are thinking about this world. Iranian leaders are thinking about the next."

Victor thought a moment. "So our largest problem with such extremists—in this case the Takbir—is that they believe they can help create, even bring on, the apocalypse?"

"I'm afraid so. And though the Russians don't share their belief system, they're happy to profit from that system. "

Both men were silent even as their thoughts were many

and loud. After a pause, Victor rose and began to pace across the Persian rug his mother had brought back from the Holy Land decades previously. She had bought it from an Arab man. She had always told the story of its purchase with joy. How she had sat over many cups of mint tea with Victor's father and the merchant, haggling, laughing, and finally settling on a price that made everyone happy.

With the toe of his shoe, Victor traced one of the carpet's swirling, white florals to where it ended in a field of blue. "How does Israel make peace with nations who have a history of saying they love death as much as we love life?"

Asher finished his coffee. "If Israel laid down our arms today and said, 'Let's have peace,' we'd be destroyed. If the Arabic nations did the same, guess what? There would be peace in the Middle East. Bottom line? The extremists want us dead. If they didn't, we'd have peace."

Victor looked up. "If our enemies come together for death, the Overcomers must come together for life. The question is, how?"

OLD JAFFA, ISRAEL

Ma'ayan started to run after the van but immediately realized the preposterousness of that. She sprinted back to the car, picking the keys out of the hummus, trying to think what needed to happen next. Mindlessly she tossed the remaining food bags into the car. Think, girl, think!

No one seemed to have seen anything. The only people in sight were walking in the opposite directions.

Rebekah had yelled out "The spine." What on earth had she meant?

Thinking wasn't working. Ma'ayan found herself praying aloud, Shafiq's story from Passover returning to her. Aloud she asked, "Give me the solution!"

Yola's face popped into her mind. What? Why was she

thinking of...? Oh. She yanked open her purse, fished for her wallet, and pulled it out: the little card Yola had given her. She dialed the number.

A man's voice immediately answered in Hebrew. "Yes."

"A woman named Yola gave me your number, said you'd help if I needed anything in Israel. My friend was just taken. Right off the street. They just took her..."

"Where are you?"

Ma'ayan described her location on the Promenade at the base of the Ha Midron Garden.

"Stay. I'll be right there."

Ma'ayan wondered if she should call the police. She didn't even know the number of the police. Plus, Rebekah was Shin Bet, which meant what, exactly?

She had barely wiped the hummus off of the keys before she heard a familiar sound: the engine of a Triumph. A man pulled up next to her and lifted the visor of his helmet, "Get on."

It was Shafiq.

Chapter Twenty-nine

H EY, MOM."

"Eitan! Are you OK?"

"Yeah, of course. Are you OK? It's almost 2:00. Where are you? We're starving!"

Ma'ayan exhaled. "You'll need to get back to Safta Liya's. Something happened. Is Jason right there?"

"Yeah. Everything alright?"

"Not exactly. Can you hand him the phone?"

Ma'ayan heard the sound of people at the beach. People who could lie beneath the sun and only worry about whether they had reapplied sunscreen. She envied them.

"Ma'ayan?"

"Jason. I don't know how to say this."

"Where's Rebekah?"

"Someone took her." Ma'ayan's voice began to wobble. The weight of the day was starting to become tangible. That and a new worry. Had it begun while riding behind Shafiq on the Triumph looking for black vans? Or when she asked him about the flash drive she had brought to Israel? Or had the vague, gut-worry begun when Shafiq arrived to the scene only seconds after Rebekah had been taken?

No, she didn't have nice, simple worries like whether or not she'd get skin cancer from the Mediterranean sun. She had the complicated kind. Like whether her friend was alive or dead and whether or not the man she was attracted to was who he said he was.

Shafiq was watching her now as she called. Her head

was swirling, and Jason was asking her something over the phone.

"I'm sorry, what?"

"Get back to Liya's. I'll meet you there. Eitan is fine."

"Thank you. I'm sorry. I'm…"

"Ma'ayan, you had nothing to do with this. At least you were there. It's better than if no one had been there. If she had just disappeared."

This time it was his voice that began to crack. He hung up.

Ma'ayan sighed, thankful at least that Jason didn't blame her. Silently, she reminded herself to breathe and to use her skills to remember every detail of the kidnapping. Anything might help.

Shafiq was waiting. "I'll take you back to Rebekah's car and follow you home."

"You notified the Shin Bet? What else can we do?

"Yes. I've done all that can be done. Now we wait. And pray."

•ٱ•

Shafiq had gone, and Eitan had gone to bed. Jason decided to camp out in the front garden in case anyone else among them was a target.

Liya tapped Ma'ayan on the shoulder and pointed to the back garden. In Hebrew, she said, "Come. You need to talk. I'm good at listening."

Ma'ayan shook her head. "I can't even think, let alone talk."

Liya put a fist on her hip.

Ma'ayan smiled despite herself and followed her nimble grandmother out into the moonlight. The lemon and olive trees cast shadows across the section of pebbles and deck. The women pulled four chairs away from the table—one for each to sit on and one for each to rest her feet on. Ma'ayan also pulled a pillow from the hammock to hold. She needed something—anything—to cling to.

Liya said, "The older you get, the more you remember to rest."

"I must be getting younger, then."

Liya leveled a look at Ma'ayan. She watched her granddaughter's face a moment before saying, "Problems will come when you're young and when you're old. When you're young you let them define you. When you're old you can choose to define them."

"What if you've had so many problems that your entire life is constantly delayed?"

"What if God trusted you to overcome your problems so that you can help others overcome theirs?"

"Well, that's nice and encouraging."

"Truly. If you are weak, how do you build muscle? You lift heavy things. You tear down what is weak to build up strength. You're a heavyweight, Ma'ayan."

Ma'ayan started laughing. She laughed until she choked and another thought came to her. "What if I helped the wrong people?"

Liya looked at her. "What do you mean?"

Ma'ayan shook her head. "I don't know. I'm tired. I can't think."

"That's a great time to pray."

"My prayers don't seem to be getting many answers these days."

"Close your eyes."

"I'll fall asleep."

"Shhh. Close your eyes."

Ma'ayan finally did as she was told. With one sense closed, her other senses opened. She felt the cooling air on her cheeks. Tasted the bourekas she'd been anticipating when she and Rebekah bought them, but which she had eaten without joy when everyone had reconvened at the house.

Liya's voice was soft now, like the breeze in the olive leaves. "Picture a door. You knock, it opens. You step inside, but you are not inside: you have stepped into another world. Here, you feel no separation. You just keep walking forward. As you do, you keep growing into your dreams, into the person you are meant to be. That walking, that process makes you an Overcomer. Keep walking."

In her heart, Ma'ayan said to that place, that presence, "Show me the doors. Be with me as I open them. Help me knock—not knock them down."

She laid her head on the back slats of the weathered wood chair. She felt the gap between two pieces of wood, felt her hair fill it. Her cheekbones seemed to relax. She unclenched her hands and let her fingers open. She felt like she was getting a massage in the spirit, and she drifted to a borderland of consciousness. She stayed there for a minute. For an eternity.

When she opened her eyes, the moonlight had shifted. Liya was no longer sitting beside her, and a peace blew through the olive leaves and her spirit.

Chapter Thirty

A WEEK PASSED AND still no news of Rebekah. No ransom, nothing. Jason tore up the countryside. Ishay had turned the word spine inside out. Overcomers came from neighboring cities. Victor Wexler sponsored private investigators. The Shin Bet wasn't saying anything.

Nothing.

Ma'ayan did the only thing she knew how to do: she worked, and worked hard. She interviewed every Overcomer she could keep still long enough to take notes on. For one interview, she rode with a man on his way to target practice at an underground gun range and then stayed to shoot a new handgun. For another, she met a woman at a large warehouse that seemed to be a cross between a linguistics institute and a high-tech software lab. As the woman spoke Hebrew into the speech synthesis device, her words came out in Arabic—in the sound of her own voice. For still another interview, Ma'ayan sat with two men in front of multiple screens of code deciphering software, watching them take the vav and the word spine—in English and Hebrew—through any and every permutation of meaning.

Ma'ayan also tried to research the group they believed had taken Rebekah. After learning of the Takbir, Ma'ayan tried to find any mention of them at all—anywhere. But even her new Arabic sources found little to nothing. The frustration was constant.

Yet all the while, the door Liya had "led" her through stayed wide open. Ma'ayan dreamt every night, sometimes waking on the hour—3:00 A.M., 4:00 A.M.—and scrambling for her notebook to write down the details as if she was interviewing her subconscious self. Apparently, she had a lot to say.

When she wasn't interviewing or researching, Ma'ayan was writing. In the shade of Liya's trees on the strangely comfortable wooden chairs, Ma'ayan wrote and wrote. She would write from breakfast to lunch, forgetting to stretch and only doing so with a wince when Eitan came to show her his rendition of the Hebrew aleph-bet, done from memory. Within the week, he was writing Hebrew words.

Had it only been a week?

Vaguely, Ma'ayan noticed that Miriam seemed to spend every non-school hour at Liya's house, tutoring Eitan in Hebrew. When Ma'ayan remembered to look up from her smudged laptop screen to see them laughing over Eitan's mispronunciation, she was pleased. Eitan had never spent much time with girls, let alone dated any, and Ma'ayan had been worried that he was missing out on high school social life because he somehow felt he needed to take care of her.

Miriam was a good girl. And there was always an adult around, not that Ma'ayan thought they'd... The thought was so out of her norm that she laughed out loud. What was her normal, anyway?

She uploaded the attachment to her email and hit send. She rubbed her neck and arched her back. Margie had invited her to write a guest blog for Haaretz's online English edition. The finished piece was in Margie's inbox now.

Ruben had wanted to publish the article in both English and Hebrew. He had thankfully offered translation services. Ma'ayan's written Hebrew was beyond rusty. She was struggling the most with the longer piece for the print edition. How to introduce the Overcomers to the world they were helping to save? What hook would work for that massive task?

She was scanning her lede again, uncertain that it set the tone for the piece, when Eitan slapped down a lined notebook next to her with a smile. "I saw you stretch. I know you're in between thoughts. Look."

Ma'ayan blinked her eyes to adjust from pixels to ink. The pages in front of her were covered in Hebrew sentences—written by her son! He was practicing by learning to write the meaning of the letters in the letters themselves. She read that aleph meant power and unity. Bet meant sanctuary, dwelling. She found her eyes tearing up. She wasn't sure whether from emotion or eyestrain.

"Eitan, I knew you were a genius, but now I have objective proof. I can't believe you're writing this much a week and a half into the trip." She looked up to her son and squinted in mock skepticism, "You sure you haven't been studying on the sly back home?"

Miriam had joined them. In her delightfully broken English, she shook her head, "No, no. He learn so fast. Faster than I learn English. Maybe if he stays in Israel, he learn completely."

Ma'ayan tried not to smile at this transparent plug for Eitan to stay. Right now, she wanted to stay too.

A DESERT WADI NEAR THE DEAD SEA, ISRAEL

Father Da'ud had not eaten for three days. He had gone far longer without food many times in the past, so he wasn't worried, even though his stomach was. It growled again.

"Shh," he said to it, "I'm praying."

As usual, he got his prayers straight from heaven, but there were more of them recently. And a sense of urgency. He traced his morning path of intercession up and down the wadi a bit more slowly than usual. He marveled at how his spirit could feed him when no pita or pomegranates were around to do so.

The sun was just reaching into the canyon when he saw the man.

Father Da'ud squinted into the distance but did not recognize the voice or figure. The stranger approached slowly, hesitantly. He called out, "Inshallah, Father Da'ud?"

"It is I. And with whom do I speak?"

"My name is Abdul-Aziz. I bring you food."

The man came closer, and Father Da'ud could see he wore a large backpack. He also noticed Abdul-Aziz's skin was covered in eczema. Large splotches of pink and peeling skin stretched all the way up the man's arms. He swung off his backpack, and it landed with a thud in the dust.

Abdul-Aziz gave a shy smile. "I heard you are a man of the spirit. That you talk to Allah, and he listens to you."

"I talk to God and His Son, yes."

"His son? Are you Christian, then?"

"Yes."

Abdul-Azim's smile wilted.

Father Da'ud smiled even more, "Ah, cheer up. You will meet this Son today. Your name means 'servant of the powerful one,' yes?"

"Yes."

"Do you have water in your pack?"

"Yes." The man bent over and reached inside, pulling out a battered metal flask of water and handing it to Father Da'ud.

The prophet accepted it with a slight bow. "How long have you had this skin condition?"

"Since I was a child."

"And you came to me hoping I could heal it? You brought me all of this food for that, yes?"

Abdul-Azim looked down, ashamed. "And money, too. Whatever you want."

"You are lucky: I don't accept payment. I accept the gift of food. But I don't heal."

The man looked up, puzzled, "But I have heard…"

Father Da'ud unscrewed the cap to the water flask. "You have heard that people have been healed. Yes, I was present. But it was not I who healed them. It was the Son of God. He heals you now."

The prophet stepped forward and doused the unsuspecting man with water. Abdul-Azim was so surprised he just stood there dripping for several seconds before anger flushed his cheeks.

Abdul-Azim wiped his brow, looking ready to strike. "Why do you mock me like this, old man?"

Father Da'ud was smiling, drinking the rest of the water. He returned the flask to the man who snatched it back, looking as if he wanted to strike Father Da'ud with it. As the man tried to calm himself, he noticed his outstretched arm. The skin was clear—no trace of the scaling, pink skin that he had known his entire life. He dropped the water flask and held up his other arm. Also clear. He ripped off his shirt, pulled up the legs of his pants, the tears already stippling the dust at his feet.

He fell to his knees in front of Father Da'ud, laughing and weeping at the same time. The old man laid his hand on Abdul-Azim's head, which was bobbing up and down in a frenzy of emotion.

Father Da'ud said, "Today you finally understand what your name means."

Smiling, the prophet sat down next to the healed man. He reached inside the pack, pulled out a bag of figs, and began to eat.

Chapter Thirty-one
Tel Aviv, Israel

MIRIAM WAS PEERING over Eitan's shoulder at his laptop—just one of many electronic devices spread across Liya's dining room table. Ma'ayan walked past the teenagers on her way to pour another glass of mint tea.

Eitan had come to Israel with a half-empty suitcase of clothes but a carry-on bulging with devices requiring cables. Ma'ayan had insisted he bring more than two t-shirts and a pair of shorts.

Ma'ayan filled her glass with ice and poured the steeped mint water over them. "What are you two staring at?"

Miriam looked up, smiling with her whole face. "Eitan teaches me computer things."

Eitan kept his eyes on the screen, "Kind of like a teaching exchange, Mom. Miriam was spending so much time teaching me Hebrew, I felt like I should do something in return."

Ma'ayan sipped the mint, letting the cool of it run through her teeth. "Sounds fair. And what's the current lesson?"

"Code."

Ma'ayan waved her free hand in the air, dismissively. "That's where you lose me. I like it when you people who know that stuff make it easy for the rest of us. Don't make me look behind the scenes. Or pages. Or whatever."

Eitan laughed, finally looking up. "Don't worry, Mom.

That's what I'm here for. It's basically just problem solving. You solve problems with words, I solve problems with program code."

Miriam poked him on the shoulder. "And I solve hunger with dinner, so now we study Hebrew. You learn food words today." She pushed away from the table and came toward the kitchen as Ma'ayan was leaving it. The girl had more spunk in her than Ma'ayan had thought. Good for her.

She left the two to dinner prep and linguistics, returning to her room. She grabbed her notebook and opened the double doors that led into the front garden. She sat in the shade of the lemon tree, thinking with her pen:

Shafiq came by again this morning. He's been checking in ever since Rebekah's capture, but I haven't exactly been friendly. Something's off there; I know it. I wanted to ask Jason if he thought it was possible Shafiq wasn't what he said he was, but I can see how close they are as friends. If and when I say something, I'll need proof, not hunches.

I keep thinking about the moon. And I keep trying not to think about the moon. It's up there, invisible behind the blue of day.

What am I not seeing?

It was immediate. The lemon trees and blue sky turned into walls and ceiling. She found herself standing behind a row of filing cabinets in a large room lit by fluorescent lights. She didn't move—she wasn't sure she could move if she wanted to, and she didn't want to know that limitation.

At least her sight and hearing worked. She could hear voices from a far corner of the large room—voices speaking in Arabic.

She was partially hidden where she stood. She could see the back of one man who faced another. The man whose face she could see wore a kuffiya and was shaking his head.

Ma'ayan's sense of smell worked too. The large room smelled of old papers and stale air, as if the air conditioner was stuck, waiting to reach a set thermostat temperature before kicking in.

She tried moving her toes. Yes, they moved. Her pulse was certainly moving. How did I get here? Where is here? She had the feeling she shouldn't be seen. She realized she was still holding the pen she had been writing with when... when whatever happened had happened.

The two men finished their conversation, and the one in the kuffiya turned to leave. The second man turned to watch him go.

Ma'ayan squinted. You've got to be kidding.

HAARETZ HEADQUARTERS, TEL AVIV

Ruben sighed, taking off his glasses and rubbing the bridge of his nose. The young intern was waiting for his response.

Ruben put his glasses back on and gave it: "If you really wanted to boycott Israel, you'd have to give up your laptops, anti-virus software, cell phones, hybrid and electric cars, solar power plants. And that's not even getting into the fields of medicine and humanitarian aid."

Ruben flipped through the young man's article. "Always show both sides of the story. At a minimum, you'll save yourself a few of the hundreds of emails sent by irate readers who will disagree with you."

The intern frowned. "I thought that op-ed pieces meant that I could present my views—"

Ruben held up a hand. "When you've lived long enough to see both sides of the story, then you can try writing about just one side because one, you'll be less inclined to do so, and two, you'll be less emotional and vehement. I can't publish this."

Ruben handed the papers back. "Look, there is a reason

we have more reporters per readership than any other newspaper in the world. There is also a reason Israel is always under attack by just about everyone. Figure out the link between those two thoughts and get back to me."

The intern finally accepted his rejected article and rose to leave. He was trying not to sulk at failing.

"Cheer up, kid. Someday soon you'll be glad this didn't get published."

When he was alone, Ruben returned to the file he'd been reading when interrupted. It was from the Israeli-American journalist he'd been in contact with. Ma'ayan Bracha wrote well; Margie had been enjoying her English blogs.

But Ma'ayan had a challenge ahead of her: the piece she'd proposed for the print version. Ruben knew full well how difficult it was to explain who and what the Overcomers were. In a world so anchored to the visible, talking about the invisible always raised more than eyebrows.

Ma'ayan had queried about describing what the world would call superpowers: miracles they would call anomalies; prophecies they would call hunches. She wrote that she, and probably some of the reading public, could believe these things happened. Everyone would have a harder time with some of the other things: raising people from the dead, transporting from one place to another.

"Such stuff," she had written, "must be experienced to be believed."

Chapter Thirty-two
Ariel, Israel

MA'AYAN BLINKED. THE man was Shafiq. He has an uncanny knack of appearing places, she thought.

Shafiq was still watching the direction the other man had left. A banner hung on the wall over the door with the Star of David slashed through and Arabic words spray-painted across it.

Ma'ayan's heart was now racing, not just because she had apparently been transported somewhere that definitely was not the front garden, but because she was right. Shafiq did work for the other side. The men had been speaking Arabic. The banner, the very mood of this room, was anti-Israel.

That meant Shafiq was dangerous. He was maybe even— she almost choked—responsible for Rebekah's capture. She felt ill and started to sink to the ground but caught herself. She couldn't let him see her.

How could she leave wherever this was without being seen or taken herself?

She looked at the labels on the filing cabinets near her. She couldn't read the Arabic script, but some of the labels were in English as well. With one eye on Shafiq and one eye busy playing journalist, Ma'ayan caught her breath. She saw the word Takbir.

Ma'ayan's spirit, mind, and body were spinning. She was trying to stand and breathe and think, and she could only seem to do one at a time. All of a sudden, she found her lips silently forming words she did not know.

She could breathe.

A peace ran through her limbs.

She could stand.

She kept forming those words.

Time—in whatever place or reality this was—stopped.

In her mind's eye, she saw a vessel—an ancient clay lamp filled with oil. She remembered seeing similar lamps in the shop windows of Jerusalem as a young girl. The vessel oil was being poured over Shafiq, but she could feel the warm oil running down her forehead. She knew: This was the anointing of favor, of destiny, of purpose. It seemed so real, she wondered if Shafiq could feel it in some way.

He still hadn't seen her. He began to speak aloud, in English. Vaguely, from what now felt like a separate realm of her being, her mind, Ma'ayan wondered: English? Why would he speak in English?

Ma'ayan realized her own lips were still moving in silent prayer. She stopped now and listened to his words.

"I walk in favor with God and man. I have the mind of Christ. I walk in supernatural intelligence."

No one but Ma'ayan was around to hear him.

Shafiq turned toward the door the other man had used. He kept speaking, "God's will be done on earth as it is in heaven."

He opened the door just as the air conditioner came on, which caused a kind of suction on the door that made him have to pull harder. Ma'ayan heard one last line before he left: "Overcomers will live up to our name."

Only now, Ma'ayan wasn't just hearing the words, she was seeing them. Her spirit saw them being sucked into the air ventilation system. And then, somehow being multiple places at once, she saw those words getting pumped through the air vents and being released throughout the building with the forced air.

She saw the words falling on men sitting in front of computers. The words bounced off of some and fell into others. The words swirled around cables and chairs, through windows and doors, into offices and hearts, upstairs and down.

It hit her: the power of her words. She, too, had the ability to alter the atmosphere around her just like an air conditioning system in a building. She could speak, could write, and change the atmosphere of not just a room, but a city. Maybe even the world.

A layered knowing folded across her—that talents and passions led toward purpose. That the Overcomers knew how to harness their talents and passions and join together in a corporate purpose. She had been wondering why she felt unfulfilled, even when she thought she was living her destiny: It had been solo. Yes, she was meant to write and always had been, but it was for what she wrote and for whom that she hadn't understood.

She closed her eyes as the words continued to enter her, to fuse with her bloodstream, to go cellular. She felt the air conditioning vent blowing her hair into her face.

When she opened her eyes, she was sitting beneath her grandmother's lemon tree in the evening wind. She still held the pen in her hand. Her notebook lay in her lap where she had left it. In it were written pages and pages of new words she didn't remember writing. The pages were translucent with the oil that was still dripping from her forehead.

ARIEL, ISRAEL

There were no windows in this room. Even with the single vent in the ceiling, it felt airless. Rebekah looked at the man who stood over her in the dark.

Azzam said, "I am sure you want to go home. We haven't been treating you like the staff does at The King David Hotel. I think their pillows are softer than my men's hands."

She didn't respond, though her body clenched in acknowledgment.

"And I am sure the Wexler's want you home as well, especially the junior Mr. Wexler."

She tried not to let her face give any trace of emotion. She knew what they knew. They still didn't know what she did. She had to keep it that way. And she could, as long as they didn't have Jason; as long as he didn't become bait, she could endure anything.

Azzam sighed. "I don't like spending too much time in here. It's rather stifling, don't you think?"

Rebekah resisted the urge to scratch the never-ending itch of her ankles covered in rusty shackles.

Azzam continued. "I thought the Overcomers had superpowers. Don't you commune with your God, and doesn't He give you the ability to move mountains?"

He leaned closer. "Aren't you supposed to see what others can't see and do what others can't? Aren't you a large threat to the Takbir—to followers of Allah?"

He stood back and tilted his head. "No. I am beginning to think you are not. Tell me the code you used to track our virus, and you can go back to your substandard religion knowing it is a lie."

Rebekah held his gaze neutrally.

Her captor shrugged his shoulders. "You choose to stay here? That is your choice. Me, I'm going to have dinner. And it will be much better than that stale slice of pita."

He gave her the kind of smile a parent gives a child who chooses to disobey and accepts her punishment. He turned and closed the door, leaving Rebekah alone again in the dark.

Chapter Thirty-three
Tel Aviv, Israel

M'AYAN FLIPPED THROUGH the pages of her notebook. It was all there: the rest of her article. And it was good. She had acknowledged her vulnerability so she could write with strength and had admitted her doubts to write with faith.

She remembered Rebekah yelling out "The spine!" when she had been captured. Ma'ayan heard that word in her head every few hours. She scrawled the title of her article: "The Spine of Faith."

She stood, stepped from the front garden into her room, grabbed her laptop, and began transcribing her own words at a furious pace.

She kept writing. She wrote of hope and power. She wrote with hope and power. She added to the words that had been given to her. Given—there was no other way to put it. She harnessed her inner skeptic to her hopeful spirit, and, as one team, they pulled the text forward.

Ma'ayan lost all track of time. She vaguely wondered if her out-of-body experience had happened inside or outside of current time. And was it even out-of-body? She'd been in her body. Her body had just popped up somewhere else.

She paused. Where was that place? Was it in Israel? It was certainly the Middle East. All those files with Arabic writing. And Shafiq had been there. Something told her he

had been there in real time, real body. If so, it was probably Israel.

In fact, she'd just seen Shafiq that morning. The transfer,
transport—whatever it had been—was so bursting with
significance that she knew there was more to remember.
It was a different kind of memory—not chronological but
cyclical and immediate.

Letting her fingers rest from her worn laptop keys,
Ma'ayan closed her eyes, remembering the moment when
Shafiq's words had entered the air conditioning ducts and
had blown through that building, wherever it was.

She tried to follow his last line as it coursed through
parts of the building she hadn't physically been in but had
seen.

Overcomers will live up to our name.

She watched the words flowing through every floor of
the building, down into—

There was a knock at the door, "Ma'ayan? Dinner is
ready."

Miriam's voice broke the moment, and Ma'ayan lost
the glimpse of something she hoped was not vital. "Start
without me."

Ma'ayan kept writing as the sun slowly faded and her
laptop screen became the only light in her room. When
she heard the front door close after Miriam left for the
evening, Ma'ayan started editing.

Liya called "goodnight" about the time that Ma'ayan
hit "save" for the third time without having made further changes. The article was done. She stretched, hearing
Eitan in the hallway.

She opened her door, "Hey, you. Want to go for a walk?"

Eitan laughed. "At eleven? Sure. I guess that means the
article is done?"

Ma'ayan rubbed her eyes, exhausted but thrilled. "It's

pretty darn great, I think. I'll read it again first thing in the morning, and then you can see it."

"My mother the perfectionist."

Ma'ayan was slipping on her sandals from a line of neatly laid out shoes belonging to Liya. She had forgotten how orderly her grandmother was and made a mental note to make sure that she left things as she found them, even when she got sidetracked with work.

Ma'ayan stood, bringing her pixel-thick brain back to the present, to her son. "Perfectionist? No. I've decided to swap my perfectionism for excellence. Life's too short to worry about perfect."

Eitan held the door for her and closed it behind them as they started down the garden walk.

They exited the garden gate and began walking along the quiet, residential street. Small cars found impossible parking spaces up to and on the sidewalks, making it difficult to walk side by side. Mother and son walked in the middle of the deserted street, moving through the orange orbs cast by the street lights.

Eitan poked his mother on the shoulder. "You missed Miriam's schnitzel."

Ma'ayan's stomach lurched in dismay. "Leftovers?"

"Of course. We knew you'd surface someday."

"No skeleton of a journalist found bent over her laptop, hmmm?"

Eitan laughed. "Not as long as I'm around to keep an eye on you."

"You. My far too grownup son." Ma'ayan stopped in the center of a circle of streetlight and threw her hands in the air. "Wait! You're going to be eighteen in a week! What happened to time?"

"Mom, you're going to wake up your neighbors."

Ma'ayan grabbed her son's shoulders in mock despair,

lowering her voice but speaking with a Yiddish accent, "Oy vey! My son! Can you forgive your mother? She has forgotten this most special day!"

Eitan was laughing. He shook off Ma'ayan's hands and steered her back down the street. "Easy. I've learned to work your distraction and guilt to my advantage."

In her normal voice, Ma'ayan said, "Not that you usually use this advantage. What's your plan?"

"Jerusalem for my birthday. A day trip."

"Deal."

"What, not even a moment's hesitation?"

"Nope. 'Cause I was just thinking you hadn't even seen the holy city. Everything's been a bit crazy. So it's a deal. Jerusalem it will be."

"Hey, cool. And today I even learned the word for 'it will be.' Actually, it's the meaning one of the Hebrew letters makes."

He drew a hook shape in the air with his finger. "When you attach the hook-shaped letter to a verb, it turns it from the past to the future or the opposite—from the future to the past. So hoiya means 'it was,' but v'hoiya means—"

"It will be." Ma'ayan looked at her son in the dark. The streetlights were thinner here.

Eitan nodded. "Like the word yehi means 'let there be light.' Or 'there will be light.'"

Ma'ayan stopped now, as Eitan continued his explanation, "Add the vav, and it means 'there was light.'"

She looked off into the darkness as if she could see her thoughts hiding there.

The vav—the hook. The hook between heaven and earth. She had been writing about the Overcomers, who felt called to bring heaven to places of darkness. To change lives. Her thoughts began to tumble over and under each other in blocks of verbs. Prepare. Align. Fight. Wait. Realign. Influence.

She looked at her son, started to speak, then looked around her.

Most of the houses were dark, only house number lights glowed faintly. But the house they stood in front of had a basement whose lights were shining onto the street, making her feet visible.

Even in the dark, Eitan recognized his mother's concentration. He waited. She looked from the basement to her son's face. She shook her head, rattling around the memory of Shafiq's words falling down through that building, wherever it was. She remembered now: The words had also fallen into the basement, into a dark room where a woman sat. Ma'ayan knew that woman.

She looked at Eitan. "Rebekah. I think I know where Rebekah is."

Ma'ayan grabbed her son's hand and started running back toward the house.

Chapter Thirty-four
Fort Worth, Texas

THE WIDE TEXAS sky had been filling with clouds all morning, and now the thunder was starting.

Della loved a good storm. She figured it meant something was brewing in the heavens. She stepped off her porch into her garden. The wind sent her hydrangeas swirling and dancing on their stems. Della started to dance with them, interceding for the Overcomers in Israel.

Something was about to break through—she could feel it. She sashayed through the big, fat blossoms, dancing with them, occasionally grabbing one gently and turning it into a temporary dance partner. Her skirts slapped against her solid thighs as her legs moved with the grace of a woman who knew her moves.

A lightning bolt hit above the far field, followed by shattering thunder. Della clapped her hands, "That's right, let it out! I speak to the four winds, I say release!"

Release. That was the word for the unction that had been with her all week. That was the word the sky was speaking.

"Release!" she yelled again into her swaying flowers. The day smelled of heat and waiting rain, of soil and blossom and all the things the wind could carry.

Della took the stem of the tallest hydrangea, held it at arm's length, and waved it in time with her hips. A series of lightning bolts hit the clouds, shooting their gray bellies with electric light, and then disappearing to another boom of thunder.

This breakthrough was going to happen. She wished she knew what it was, but she had been praying too long to worry about hearing all the results. Her confidence was sourced far beyond a confirmation.

She released the flower, bowing, "Thank you, most skinny gentleman. You make a fine partner."

As she straightened back up, the first drops of rain started to fall on the dance floor of her windy garden.

Ariel, Israel

Rebekah still had her eyes closed. She was more at peace than she had been for however long she had been in this dark cell. She sent Jason thoughts of joy, hope, and love. She thought of the ring she had shown Ma'ayan—imagined Jason placing it on her finger. The finger that was now swollen and bruised.

She began singing the Hava Nigila, a song she had sung with others at many weddings and one she hoped to hear at her own celebration:

Let us rejoice

Let us rejoice

Let us rejoice and be happy

Let us sing

Let us sing

Let us sing and be happy

She started to laugh. The laughter wouldn't leave. It persisted until she was shaking with it.

No—the room was shaking. She stopped singing. The floor was definitely shaking. Floor, walls, room.

Earthquake.

Well, if this was the way she'd go, she'd go singing. She continued the song, louder now:

Awake, awake, brothers!

Awake brothers with a joyful heart,

Awake brothers with a joyful heart,

Awake brothers with a joyful heart!

The movement of the earth and the building caused her voice to quiver. To not let the words be drowned out by the rumblings, Rebekah sang the last lines at the top of her lungs:

Awake brothers, awake brothers

With a joyful heart!

As quickly as it had come, the quaking left. The room filled with silence. Rebekah felt a peace so thick she couldn't feel the chains on her ankles.

Curious, she wiggled her feet as best she could. Strange.

She reached down and felt a chunk of the stone floor that had shifted up, busting the connection of the chain to the hook embedded in the ground. That almost made sense. What didn't make sense was that the shackles themselves had also burst open, leaving her ankles free.

Gently and gingerly, Rebekah slid up the wall to standing, testing the weight of her legs on her feet. Momentarily dizzy, she leaned back against the humid stone behind her, catching her breath and balance.

There was more light now. She squinted and saw the door's bolt had split, leaving the door slightly ajar.

"Thank You, El Gibbor."

She stepped toward the door, curious that she could not hear sounds from any other part of the building. Hope beginning to pulse through her blood stream, Rebekah touched the door. Cautiously, she pushed it farther open.

A man stood on the other side.

Chapter Thirty-five
Havilah Gas Field, Mediterranean Sea

ZADOK GRIPPED THE stair railing, leaning toward the brightly-lit derrick in the dark. "Well?"

The driller, his haggard, grizzled face set firmly, whatever the circumstance, broke into a rare smile. "Sababa. Everything's fine."

Zakok released the railing with a whoop and clapped his hands. "Thank you, my friend. Thank you!"

The driller saluted and turned back to the derrick as Zadok started dancing a jig. The night workers laughed, and a few clapped. Everyone was relieved. When news of the quake had flashed onto his news feed, Zadok's visions of prosperity for Israel via natural gas had suspended. If anything had broken far below the sea…

But nothing had.

Zadok finished his dance, bowed to the men, and shooed them back to work. The men adjusted their hard-hats and clambered back to their posts.

Breathing heavily, Zadok looked up to the night sky. Out here on the Sea, the stars were a nightly spread of heaven. Though he often missed his wife during long stretches on the drilling platform, Zadok also missed these stars when he was back in the city.

He nodded to the constellations he could not name and whispered something no one within earshot could hear.

HAARETZ HEADQUARTERS, TEL AVIV, ISRAEL

Ruben smiled. Ma'ayan Bracha's article was perfect. Raw, universal, and personal all at once. He didn't often find something like this in his inbox—worth the late night at the office. That, and he'd been present for the quake.

He scanned his news feed and the emails from local reporters:

"Surprisingly little damage…"

"A few power outages…"

"Epicenter further in the desert, closer to Ariel…"

Ruben nodded to his screen. Let the reporters do their thing. Everyone would be able to read about the quake over breakfast. Few would pay attention to the pre-Independence Day piece they'd planned to run the next day.

He lifted his glasses and rubbed the bridge of his nose.

What had he been doing? Oh yes, Ma'ayan's article. He was tired. What time was it? Midnight? Just seeing the time made him more tired.

Ruben forwarded Ma'ayan's article to one of the translators. Now, it was time to get home to Margie, argue about windows that hopefully hadn't shattered, and go to sleep.

•ו•

Ma'ayan's phone finally rang. It hadn't finished a single ring before she answered it and said, "I think I know where she is."

Eitan was sitting next to his mother on the couch. They'd been sitting up since the earthquake, watching the news and waiting for Shafiq to call.

Shafiq simply said, "Where?"

Ma'ayan sighed. She'd forgotten the improbability of her experience. She didn't care if both Shafiq and Eitan thought she was crazy. If there was even a sliver of a chance that she could help Rebekah, she had to try.

Ma'ayan took a deep breath. "Prepare for insanity. Don't ask me questions 'til I'm done. If what I say makes even a drop of sense to you, please go with it."

"Done."

"Let's just say I had a vision. I saw you in the…" Ma'ayan hesitated. What if his phone was tapped? Or hers? Or, and she hadn't thought of it until this moment, there was a bug somewhere in her grandmother's house?

She tried not to swear aloud. Eitan was watching her with his ridiculously mature mix of patience and skepticism.

She sighed. Choose your words well. That's what you do for a living. You can do this.

To Shafiq, she said, "You know that sometimes knowledge doesn't come naturally. Suffice it to say, I think she is being held in a basement room of a building you know about."

There was a brief silence.

"If you know about me being in this building, why are you calling me?"

"Because I was…given a vision of this building where I heard a certain moon-lover say that a certain group 'will live up to their name.' His words flowed through the air conditioning ducts into the room where a missing friend is being held. That's where I saw her."

Eitan's patience had faded and skepticism remained, turning his face into a question mark. He mouthed, "Mom? Are you crazy?"

Ma'ayan waved his question away and stood, waiting for Shafiq's answer. "Well?"

"The moon isn't just beautiful; she's wise."

Chapter Thirty-six

Ariel, Israel

JALIL WAS CONFUSED. What was the woman doing, standing at the door? Before thinking, he asked in Arabic, "How did you get out of your chains?"

Rebekah, giddy with release, didn't register Jalil as a threat. Somehow, she knew this was a moment for his spirit. Unafraid, she smiled, mentally telling her body to start pumping adrenaline.

In Arabic, she responded, "God opened them for me. It's not so strange; He's done it before. Read the book of Acts."

While Jalil was still registering what she said, Rebekah struck him on the side of his neck, just enough to knock him out for as long as it would take to get out of wherever she was.

Jalil slumped to the ground and landed in a fold of robes.

Rebekah breathed to regain her balance. "That part wasn't in the Scripture, but I'm ad-libbing."

She felt lightheaded. She was going to need more than adrenaline. She stood a moment, gathering strength, thinking.

She'd seen Jalil before. He was the doubter. He hadn't wanted to participate in her capture and had even brought her figs and dates over the last week, as if he could atone for his role in her imprisonment. By hitting him, she'd relieved him of the burden of preventing her escape. His punishment would likely be less severe.

A single bulb hung in the ceiling several yards away. Rebekah began to feel her way down the dimly-lit hall. A stairwell emerged from the far end.

Just as she took the first step up, she saw a pair of legs coming down.

A DESERT WADI NEAR THE DEAD SEA, ISRAEL

A small chunk of the steep wadi rock face broke off far above Father Da'ud. He was walking a rough outline of Russia, deep in prayer for government officials and didn't want to be interrupted. The rock began to rattle its way down into the shaded ravine, breaking into smaller and smaller pieces, some of which narrowly missed him as he closed the southwest border of the dusty "map" with his feet.

A few of the dislodged rocks rolled to a stop not far from where Israel would be in Father Da'ud's imaginary geography. He stepped over the rocks and looked up, blinking at the bright sky. He squinted, looked down, then back up. He laughed out loud.

Arms outstretched, head back, and beard lifting high, Father Da'ud began to sing at the top of his lungs. He sang ancient songs that few alive would know. Songs that stir men and women to acts of faith and courage. He stood there singing until his voice cracked and his throat felt dry, and then he started his regular laps of intercession, hands clasped behind his back, eyes on the ground but seeing the heavens.

ARIEL, ISRAEL

Rebekah stopped at the sight of the feet. The feet stopped, too. She had used all of her energy to knock out the man in the hallway. She had just enough strength to ascend the stairs, not to deal with whoever might be on them.

She did the only thing she could do. She gathered her spirit together, connected with heaven, and prayed it to her circumstance.

The feet started moving again. Then legs beneath a white thawb appeared on the stairs. Then a torso. Then...

She whispered, "Shafiq!"

He came toward Rebekah carrying a bundle of white fabric, glancing at Jalil on the ground. He gave her a quick hug that she had to keep herself from collapsing into.

He shook out the fabric as he asked, "You can walk?"

"Yes." She accepted the thawb and struggled to pull it on over her filthy clothing. Shafiq helped her pull it past her waist, and then began wrapping her head in a kuffiya.

That reminded her. She pointed to the fallen man. "His name is Jalil. He was the only one who showed me any kindness."

Shafiq responded by dragging the man into the cell and closing the door on him.

He looked at Rebekah. "Most of the men are out assessing damage done to the satellites. We only have a few minutes. We're going to just walk out of here. There's a gatehouse. The guard will have to open the gate for us, so I'll say we're checking the secondary generator at the outer fence. Stay behind me, head down. Your face is dirty and bruised enough that they might not immediately notice you are a woman."

"Gee, thanks."

He gave half a smile and started up the stairs. Rebekah kept close behind him. The rough brown stone of the basement gave way to a gray cinderblock ground floor. Shafiq led Rebekah through bare and sterile halls, past a room filled with filing cabinets dimly lit by a single bulb.

Somewhere in the day-to-day part of her brain, Rebekah reminded herself to not complain about the Shin Bet's décor again to Mr. Ben-Ami. She almost laughed. How could she think of interior design while her kidneys still ached from the last beating the men had given her?

They passed a room of computers where three men were arguing and pointing to screens. No one paid any attention to the two robed figures.

Rebekah prayed they'd be unseen. She didn't have to ask with words; her whole bruised body prayed for her: Let us be unseen. Help us escape. The peace was still with her. That bliss-buzz of inexplicable peace.

Shafiq reached an outer door and stopped. Rebekah caught her breath. Another man yanked the door open and entered, making eye contact with neither of them, muttering under his breath.

Shafiq looked back at the retreating man, then at Rebekah. He raised an eyebrow and continued through the outer door. The two crossed a dusty brown court-yard, staying to the shadowed side, away from the single stadium light mounted to one of the outer walls. Shafiq headed toward the gatehouse adjacent to a massive iron gate. The gate was the only way in or out of the compound.

A man emerged from the gatehouse holding a glass of coffee, a large rifle slung across his shoulder. He stepped under a hanging light above the door and cast a short shadow on the dirt. He poked at a crack in the wall with his finger before scratching his head.

Shafiq greeted him in Arabic, "Inshallah. I must check the outer generator."

The guard turned toward him and took a sip of his coffee. He looked at Shafiq and then around him, his eyes seeing right through Rebekah as if she weren't there. "It's a heavy gate to lift off the shed. You'll probably need two people."

Shafiq looked at the guard and then where Rebekah stood. She blinked at him deliberately, trying to speak to his spirit that her prayer had been answered.

Shafiq looked back at the guard, lifted the cuff of his thawb high up his arm to reveal a massive bicep. He flexed. It bulged.

Then the guard's eyes also bulged. "Maybe you can lift it alone." He ducked inside the guardhouse and released the gate. It started to slide open. To anyone looking from the building's windows, it appeared Shafiq left alone.

Chapter Thirty-seven

Tel Aviv, Israel

MUHAMMED KHAN STIRRED himself a glass of Turkish coffee. He was up this late; he might as well start the day. Plus, he sensed he was on the brink of cracking the code.

Still stirring, he walked past the stacks of old motherboards and monitors. His mind more awake than his body, he tripped over a loose cable and spilled a swath of coffee on the stained cement floor. The cat uncurled herself from her perch on a dusty printer feeder and came to investigate.

The computer tech watched his cat sniff the spilt coffee before she continued to her food bowl. As he stared at the shape of the stain, he realized it was in the shape of a vav. Muhammed Khan remembered Shafiq's story of the dead professor and the letter vav. He remembered his own last conversation with Professor Uziel. That wise man, though not a computer programmer, had understood the nature of code. He had worked with the Shin Bet and had an uncanny way of making connections among anything— even things he didn't know about. Connections.

Muhammed Khan turned quickly back toward his crammed work desk, resting his now half-empty coffee in a crevice formed by a deconstructed hard drive and a broken keyboard.

He lifted down the chipped clay bowl where he kept the flash drive the American-Israeli woman had brought and inserted the USB end into his main computer.

The files popped up. He scanned, found what he was looking for, and opened the file. This just might work.

•ֿ ן •

Ma'ayan couldn't sleep. Shafiq had promised he'd call as soon as he had Rebekah to a safe place—if he found her. If.

Eitan had gone to bed. She turned the TV off, went out into the back garden, and began pacing, barefoot, on the small stones beneath the olive tree.

Her phone jingled. A text from Shafiq. "She is safe."

It must have been close to two in the morning, but Ma'ayan yelled, "Yes!" at the top of her lungs. Her voice echoed off of the stone wall and reverberated among the leaves.

She called Jason. She called everyone whom she knew to be involved in Rebekah's release. When she ran out of numbers, she stood still on the gravel, the cool of deep night entering into her toes, her arches, her soles.

Della. She dialed the number, and before the phone had even rung, Della answered, "Oh goody, this time I get to hear the story."

TEL AVIV, ISRAEL

Mrs. Uziel stood at the door of her late husband's office. She loved the lamplight glowing across the spines of books and polished wood. She loved the memory of her husband, bent over his desk, deep in a world of words. Many times, she had stood where she was now, watching him in that world of spirit he'd get lost in—unaware of her presence until she announced a meal or a visitor.

She walked over to his desk and sat in his chair, smelling the leather as her body warmed it. She leaned over his desk, over the books she'd left as he'd left them. She rested her forehead forward onto the open page of a wide book, feeling the softness of the thick pages and the weight of her own head on them.

Minutes passed. It was an oddly comforting pose, as if bowing to the life her husband had led. She felt her face relax, her neck relax. When she lifted her head, her forehead stuck to the page, and it turned open to the next.

She saw a thin slip of paper near the spine. On it were notes from a Rabbi Shmuel with whom Leo had often met. There was a sketch of the human spine next to the letter vav. Nearest the spine was written "The Divine Name." Nearest the vav were two arrows: one pointing up to the words upper realm and the other pointing down to the words lower realms. The Rabbi had written the Shemoneh Esrei, the Prayer of Eighteen, with an arrow pointing back toward the spine and a marginal jot explaining that it was the position of bowing to The Name in prayer.

Mrs. Uziel held up the paper, noticing that the Rabbi had dated it—less than a week before her husband had been killed. Her own spine began to tingle.

She remembered something. An Arab man had visited her late husband. The youngish tall one who stooped. He had visited not long after the Rabbi, and Leo had enjoyed their conversation immensely. Over dinner, he'd told his wife, "That young man is so good at what he does; I have a feeling he could program the Ten Commandments into the Internet and the world would obey."

What was that man's name? Muhammed something. It was always Muhammed something. She found her husband's calendar and looked for Rabbi Shmuel's name. Finding it, she looked through the little boxes leading up to the day Leo had…there: Muhammed Khan. And a phone number. It was late, but she reached for the phone.

•ו•

Muhammed Kahn hung up the phone, his head full of this new information. The cat leapt onto his desk surface, adroitly finding level surfaces between computer parts for her paws and stepping toward the screen with a flick of her long tail.

He was so close.

The flash drive had been loaded with a "double agent" code. It was incomplete, but the idea was that it could detect a virus and make the virus think it was part of its own system. Meanwhile, as the double agent code ran— seemingly in conjunction with the virus—it would bounce the viral code back to the originator, infecting the source computers with that which they intended to infect other computers.

Shafiq had told Muhammed Kahn about Rebekah's kidnapping and what she had yelled out just before being taken. He had asked the computer programmer whether "the spine" had anything to do with the code.

Muhammed Kahn reached over to pet the cat. She arched her back, her spine turning into a slinky crescent.

The spilled coffee. The vav. The spine. The…

The cat leapt from the desk just as Muhammed Kahn realized he'd figured out the code.

Chapter Thirty-eight

Sidney Ali Beach, North of Tel Aviv

"AMAZING WHAT THREE days can do." Rebekah lay on a beach chair beneath an umbrella with a glass of tea in hand. "From darkness to light. And especially the light at this beach."

Jason, sitting to her left, reached for her hand in the brilliant shade of full afternoon. Everything glistened—the glass of tea, the Mediterranean shore lined with swimmers, and the future.

Jason was growing a beard in preparation for another assignment. He was consciously getting as much sun as he could to darken his skin, too. Rebekah smiled at these details, squeezing his hand.

She looked out to see Ma'ayan and Eitan splashing farther down the beach in the sparkling surf. Ma'ayan's friendship, though so brief, had linked them more closely than many friendships she'd had since school.

As if to prove life would go on, they all had decided to come to the beach like they'd planned the day Rebekah had been taken.

Jason said, "I'm proud of you."

Still watching the sea, Rebekah said, "Sitting in that darkness the Takbir had created, I was so grateful I had started the process to destroy it. Funny that the honey pot was set in motion the morning I was taken."

"Yes. Mr. Ben-Ami was able to use the findings you'd set in motion to trace the virus to the Takbir. The timing

was divine; we figured that at about the moment Shafiq
got you out, Muhammed Khan had cracked the code."

Rebekah nodded. "I'm glad he passed the 'double agent'
code to Shafiq."

"Who then gave it to Mr. Ben-Ami. Me too."

"I'm proud of all the people I work with. Especially my
colleague," Rebekah smiled, "the one who is over fond of
lemon semolina cakes. He hid a key phrase in the counter
code. Call it a Shin Bet Signature."

"And the Takbir will soon discover their virus has an
antidote." Jason turned his gaze from the water to look
at Rebekah. "My question for the Shin Bet: Why is the
Takbir headquarters still full of terrorists when we know
where they are?"

Rebekah looked down. "We still need information.
Azzam alone is powerful. But he also has connections
beyond Iran that we need. The Russians who created the
code, for instance. And Shafiq has known where they were
for a while?"

Jason sighed. "Yes. I was the only one who knew. He
couldn't tell anyone—both to keep his cover and to pull
as much information as only you can when you're on the
inside. I wanted to come with him to release you. But
when emotions are involved...it was better this way."

Rebekah felt Jason's fingers wrapped around her own.
The swelling had gone down, and though she opted not
to wear a swimsuit until the bruises faded, she felt—if
not entirely looked—her normal self. The peace that had
entered her cell just before the earthquake had not left her,
even in the escape. In fact, she'd been riding high in a
kind of bliss she had never known.

Jason turned toward her, "Do you want to go to
Jerusalem for Eitan's birthday this week, or is that too
much?"

"Probably too much. Though it's quite the celebration, turning eighteen. Did you know that in Hebrew, the number eighteen means life? It is the strongest number of blessing to the people of Israel. If you want to give with the most blessing, you give in increments of eighteen."

Jason let go of her hand and shook his head, "Hmm, then that poses a problem for me."

She looked at his face to see if he was serious. "What are you talking about?"

Jason swung his legs around to reach into the beach bag he'd brought. He didn't answer, and he didn't seem to find what he was looking for, so he knelt down in the sand to look more closely.

Rebekah asked, "Did you lose something?"

He looked up and smiled. "I did, briefly, but I found her again."

He shimmied closer, knees still in the sand, and held out a small box.

Rebekah's body flushed with the tingles she'd called stars as a child. She looked at Jason, full and straight in his eyes.

He opened the box in front of her. "What does the number-twenty four mean?"

Inside the box was the ring. The ring from the Jaffa jeweler's: twenty-four karat gold filigree encasing an emerald—her Israeli birthstone from the tribe of Levi.

Rebekah couldn't speak.

Jason looked just a bit nervous. "Actually, that's not the question I planned to ask."

Rebekah found her voice and smiled so large she felt her ears pop. "That's OK. I've always planned to say yes."

She leaned across, grabbed him by the neck, and kissed him with the kiss she had dreamed of giving him while locked away in that dank, dark cell.

ARIEL, ISRAEL

Shahkam drummed his fingers on the desktop next to his keyboard. What was wrong? He had lost remote access of the trial sites, and now it seemed someone had entered his system. Shahkam's ego felt like it had been gut punched. He was one of the best. Azzam himself had brought him from Iran for this job.

Who out there was messing with him?

Shakham had spent the morning trying to figure out what had happened to the code and to fix it. At first, he hoped he could blame the mess on the Russian programmers, but he knew their virus worked. He'd been running it for almost two weeks, gathering data from highly sensitive powers in and far beyond Israel. What they had was already powerful, but it was just the beginning.

There was one more day to go until Azzam planned to launch the virus, and now this? His boss wouldn't accept failure.

Shakham stared at his computer, knowing he could do nothing more. He pushed back from his desk. Face flushed, he sulked toward Azzam's office.

When he knocked, Azzam himself opened it. He looked at the programmer's face and told him to come inside. Once he had closed the door, he asked, "What is wrong?"

"Um, sir. It seems that someone has…has compromised our virus. I no longer have control."

"What? We stopped the Shin Bet woman before she could finish tracing us. When did this happen?"

"I'm not sure how long the anti-virus has been installed. Like ours, it could have been latent for a while. But this morning, it became obviously active."

Azzam clenched the fingernails of his right hand deep into his palm until it hurt and then kept holding at that pressure.

"Sir, what about the launch?"

Azzam released his fingers and stared at Shahkam. "You will find out what happened and fix it. We will continue as planned. There is no backing down. I want full access to the Prime Minister's computer systems by the date I planned. And if you don't fix it this way, I have another way for you to take care of it...until I find someone else who can."

Shahkam didn't like the sound of that.

SIDNEY ALI BEACH, NORTH OF TEL AVIV

Shafiq and Ishay hailed Ma'ayan from farther south down the shore. Ma'ayan waved back to the approaching men. They carried bags from the market: the picnic. As they approached, Ma'ayan couldn't help noticing both men had taken off their shirts. She tried not to look at Shafiq. She had the ridiculous schoolgirl thought that Shafiq and magnifique rhymed.

She reminded herself to act her age and greeted the men as they placed the bags on the sand and approached. She smiled. "Thanks for bringing the food."

Eitan leapt from the water. "Anyone want to race to the lifeguard tower?"

Ishay laughed. "I will." He kicked off his sandals and ran headlong into the water, coming up to Eitan and saying, "Ready? Go!"

The two began splashing, their backs glistening like dolphins in the sun and water. Shafiq gave one of his rare smiles.

Ma'ayan realized that this was the first time they'd been alone since Rebekah's rescue. Shafiq turned to Ma'ayan, his smile changing to one of gentleness. "What made you trust me?"

Ma'ayan blinked and looked down at her feet just

below a shifting surface of seawater. Her heels and toes were sinking into the sand. She looked back at Shafiq. "I'll start with what made me distrust you. It took you just minutes to get to the promenade after Rebekah was captured. After that, I started to wonder. I thought the nervous feeling I had sitting next to you at Passover was my reporter instinct sensing you weren't what you said you were. But you are. That feeling was just—" Ma'ayan felt herself blush. She stopped herself from saying attraction and started to talk faster to cover her embarrassment. "So to answer your question, I started to trust you when…well, you won't believe me. But you're an Overcomer, so maybe you will. I was sitting in my grandmother's garden, and all of a sudden I was in a building I'd never seen. And I saw you."

Ma'ayan stopped, feeling like her tongue had continued to form words even after the rational part of her mind had told her to be quiet.

Shafiq's smile had shifted to one of compassion. Not the pity kind, but the expansive kind. Ma'ayan watched his face.

He watched hers, finally saying, "The darker the night, the brighter you shine."

For once, he looked hesitant, but the look disappeared as he asked, "Shall we take these to Jason and Rebekah? They shouldn't stay in the sun too long."

Ma'ayan nodded, though Shafiq carried all of the bags himself. They climbed up the soft sand diagonally, toward the couple beneath the umbrella. When they reached Jason and Rebekah, they were greeted by Rebekah holding up her hand, waving her engagement ring in the sun beyond the shade of the umbrella. The emerald caught the sun and threw back great flashes of green.

Ma'ayan smiled. It was time for new things to begin.

Chapter Thirty-nine
Jerusalem, Israel

THE FOUR WALKED two-by-two along the Via Dolorosa: Miriam and Eitan, Ma'ayan and Shafiq. The always-crowded street was even more crowded than usual. Yom Ha'atzmaut, Israel's Independence Day, had begun at sundown the night before.

The narrow passage was packed with street-front shops, and vendors were selling even more Israeli flags, prayer shawls, and Stars of David than usual. But the regular fare was also there: frankincense and myrrh in brass bowls. Spices displayed in elaborately patterned pyramids three feet high. Baskets of pomegranates big as grapefruits. Baskets of oranges hanging above and baskets of dates brimming below.

Ma'ayan stopped to marvel at buckets of electric-pink cauliflower and oily black olives, at cones of solid yogurt and scoops of fluffy saffron. The underlying air was thick with scents of sweat and bread, layered here and there with honey, sandal leather, or incense.

Eitan was taking pictures of everything—and of Miriam in front of everything. The two seemed to be an item. Ma'ayan sighed, unsure what she thought of her son falling in love for the first time. Happy? Torn? Both? And then there was the feeling that this was a double date.

Shafiq, as he seemed able to do, read her mind. Quietly, he told her, "It is a good match. Don't worry."

She looked at him, wondering if he meant her son and Miriam or himself and her.

He smiled mischievously and gently pulled her arm back as a car tried to turn a tight corner. The white scarf Della had given Ma'ayan slipped off her shoulders. She adjusted it, watching the driver reversing and forwarding as a group of pedestrians helped direct him. He looked annoyed.

Eitan and Miriam were on the other side of the car, and Eitan gestured that they'd be at a shop around the corner.

While waiting for the car to inch its way out, Ma'ayan fished inside her purse for her water bottle. When she pulled it out, the necklace Peter had given her was wrapped around the cap.

Shafiq looked at the white stone and then at Ma'ayan.

Ma'ayan held it out to him. "It was a friend's. He—he gave it to me just before he died."

"And you don't wear it." It wasn't a question, but a statement.

Ma'ayan shook her head.

Shafiq handed it back to her. "You will."

The car finally made the turn and continued, improbably, down what Ma'ayan assumed had been a pedestrian street.

When Shafiq and Ma'ayan caught up with the teenagers, Eitan was framing a picture of a gelatinous mass of candy with his phone camera. The orange stuff was lit from behind and glowing like a sweet spaceship. Passersby jostled him.

Ma'ayan poked him in the ribs. "Hey Ansel Adams, let's head toward the church and then get lunch."

Miriam clapped her hands. "Yes. I'm getting hungry."

•⁊•

Jalil knew this was the day he would die. He didn't how or for what, but the knowledge of his impending death left him unafraid.

In fact, he felt an odd peace—especially since he had a feeling he would die helping prevent one of Azzam's plans.

It all started when he read the book of Acts—or when the woman told him about it before knocking him to the floor. He didn't blame her, was thankful even. While lying there on the stones of the cell, he had been both unconscious and conscious. He couldn't move, but he could see— even with his eyes closed.

And what he had seen! The entire basement filled with a pulsing light. A being had appeared above him. Was it an angel? A god?

The being, Jalil thought it might be a "He," had leaned over Jalil and told him, "You had many chances to bring this light you see to the darkness. You have known of plans for darkness."

Still unable to move or speak, Jalil had tried to admit that he had done nothing. That he was guilty—and sorry. With his spirit, he asked the being, "What can I do? How can I make things better?"

The being smiled, "You can help me."

Even though Jalil wasn't sure who this man was, he had the feeling He didn't need anybody's help. Was this Allah? Was this his messenger?

The man answered his thoughts, "I am the one the Overcomers work with. The one whose followers you have killed and tried to kill."

A remorse crept from the stones into Jalil's robes. It entered his spirit, mind, and body. He wanted to cry out that he had wanted to stop, that he had felt a pull toward something he could not name. That if he were given a name for this desire, this deep call, he would turn toward it.

The man smiled. "I know. I know because it is I who put that desire into your heart."

Jalil wanted to weep. And though he could not yet move, he felt his heart launching through time and space, pulling out hopes from his childhood and desires for his future. He felt a knowing that brought such joy he needed no name for it.

With his spirit, Jalil asked the being, "What can I do? How can I make things better?"

"You can't, on your own. But you can partner with me. If you do, you can do things far beyond your imagination."

"Tell me what to do. I'll do it."

"I want you to know my heart. When you know my heart, you know what to do,"

Jalil thought. "I need to stop the Takbir."

The man smiled. "See? It is easy. Yes. You will be sent to Jerusalem for a terrible thing. Go. But instead of allowing this thing to happen, stop it."

"How can I stop it?"

"Protect the one who is surrounded by angels."

"Who?"

The man disappeared. Jalil's spirit vision sight faded, and he started to feel his fallen body just as Azzam found him there on the broken stones of the woman's cell.

Jalil's kuffiya had cushioned his head from the fall, Azzam said. "And a good thing. Your services are needed."

Azzam had yanked Jalil to his feet, staring around the vacant cell. "You must make this right. Know this: I don't trust you. You have to earn my trust back. Until then, consider yourself back to lackey status."

Standing in the Old City of Jerusalem, Jalil sighed. On

this job, he was just the driver. He was making something right, but not for the leader of the Takbir. Jalil was done with destruction, with hateful death. If his own death, given as sacrifice, could help end even a small part of the cycle of hate, he was willing. He almost smiled. The Takbir had been trained to carry their belief unto death. Jalil was doing that—just for the side he no longer believed to be the enemy.

He had driven Shahkam to Jerusalem. Azzam told Jalil that the young programmer had been reassigned. The normally cocky young man was rigid and silent during the entire drive from Ariel. When Jalil tried to find a parking spot on the outskirts of the city, Shahkam gestured for him to stop the car and said, "I can walk from here."

With that, Shahkam stalked off up the hill. Puzzled, Jalil watched him, waited a bit, and then started to follow him at a distance, using the thick crowds to remain unseen.

Chapter Forty

ITAN AND HIS birthday contingent continued toward the end of the Via Dolorosa toward the Church of the Holy Sepulcher. They passed more wares: long ovals of sesame-sprinkled loaves. The ubiquitous t-shirts. Ma'ayan's favorite was a smiley face with side locks that read: "Don't worry, be Jewish."

And always those worn stones beneath their feet—stones that had been there for millennia, witnesses to pivotal history.

The square in front of the church was only slightly less crowded than the Via. The four stood still to take in the façade of arches and pillars and the tourists swarming around them.

Shafiq said, "This is the site believed to be Golgotha. The place where Christ was crucified. It is also said to be the site of his tomb. The place where he was resurrected."

Ma'ayan leaned against a wall. "Some mighty history here."

To Eitan, who was taking a picture of the church, she said, "Funny how your birthday coincided with the Israeli Day of Independence, hmm? Maybe the coinciding is no coincidence." She winked.

Eitan winked back.

Miriam, for once not posing for a picture, looked up at this, "Yes, and it is the sixth day of the month of Iyar.

Eitan took his photo. "Hey, doesn't the vav also represent the number six?"

Shafiq looked away from the arches and leveled his gaze at Ma'ayan. "Professor Uziel had circled the vav…"

Ma'ayan swallowed, looking at her three companions in turn. "Do you think it's possible that the Takbir planned something for today?"

Eitan put his phone in his pocket. "Where? Here in Jerusalem?"

Shafiq nodded. "If so, it would be at a place of importance for either the Jews or Christians or both."

Ma'ayan frowned. "Maybe even more the latter. Everyone knows Islam extremists hate the Jews. But not everyone knows they hate the Americans. To the terrorists, Israel is a little evil compared to the big evil of the United States. And the United States is predominantly Christian."

Shafiq nodded. "So their target could be a Christian site. And that would be unexpected on a day celebrating Israeli heritage. Less guarded than the Temple Mount or the Wailing Wall."

Ma'ayan looked at the Church's façade, her face tightening. "Like the place where Christ is believed to have been crucified and resurrected?"

Miriam's eyes were wide, trying to follow all of the English. She was still back at the idea that something was going to happen on the sixth. "But big celebrations start yesterday. Why today?"

Shafiq was scanning the crowd, but he answered—more as if figuring things out himself than giving out information: "Because people were expecting terrorism last night—the speeches, the parades. Today is the relaxed part of the holiday. And I happen to know that the people running this group like to use attributes from their targets' languages, history, and religion against them. They would have chosen the sixth of Iyar because it relates to the number associated with the vav. And the vav that

Professor Uziel had circled was from an article about this very celebration: Independence Day!"

He ran his hand across his shaved head, putting more together. "They would have purposefully chosen a day corresponding to the number of the Hebrew aleph-bet that represents connection just so they could try to break that connection. And that little—" Shafiq tried to calm his tensing face as he thought out loud in front of an audience. "That computer programmer Shakham had already created a virus that would have taken over computers from Tel Aviv to Washington, D.C., allowing the Takbir full access to the highest level of government files. And who knows how long it would have taken for anyone to find out?"

Miriam, still baffled, looked back and forth at the other three. Eitan was deep in thought, staring at the middle of the circle the four had formed.

Ma'ayan watched Shafiq's face. "So the vav was part of the virus—even if just for the date of its planned release? The Takbir was giving new meaning to the expression 'go viral!'"

Shafiq's face finally did soften. "Yes. The vav was part of the virus. And part of the anti-virus. Though no one would have known for a while, even if they did release it today... "

Eitan looked up, brow lined in concentration as he stared off into the square at a fixed point. "The Shin Bet already figured that if we know about an anti-virus, then they could know about it now, too."

Ma'ayan nodded, "And if they do know that their planned got derailed..."

Shafiq added, "They will be angry. Angry enough to do something more physical than cyber terrorism."

"More like physical terrorism." Ma'ayan looked up and noticed Eitan was walking quickly toward the center of the square. Assuming he had found something of interest to photograph, she watched, curious to see what could have distracted him from their conversation.

A man stood still in the center of the square as people passed him in thick groups on all sides. He had a look of intense concentration and purpose. Even from this distance, Ma'ayan could tell he was sweating. Probably because he was wearing a bulky coat on a hot day.

She looked back at her son and blinked. For a strange second, it looked as if he was surrounded by angels. Her pulse quickened. "Shafiq, did you see..."

Shafiq followed Ma'ayan's gaze to see a man in a kuffiya running toward the man in the coat—or was it toward Eitan?

Shafiq started running, too. Ma'ayan froze, watching as the man in the kuffiya pushed Eitan back in the direction he'd come before jumping onto the man in the coat.

"No!" Ma'ayan screamed.

But her scream was lost in a shatter of explosion as chunks of stone shot from the square, taking flight just in time to begin their thunderous fall back to earth.

Chapter Forty-one
Ein Bokek, Dead Sea

I T HAD TAKEN weeks, but Nasser had finally found it—the hotel where General Nikolayev was staying with a Russian party. Nasser had been waiting in the lobby all morning, pretending to read the paper and hoping the Russians would come down for breakfast. They hadn't.

Nasser sighed.

Since Shafiq had prayed for him that day at the café, Nasser's entire existence had shifted from one of hopelessness to hope. If there was a God out there who could heal people, Nasser wanted to know Him. He had figured he might as well begin the acquaintance by helping the one who had introduced him to this healer: Shafiq.

And so, Nasser kept returning to the conversation he had overheard that night he'd lain drunk in the bombed-out lab, accidentally eavesdropping on plans for disaster. Nasser had replayed that night and the following afternoon sipping coffee with Shafiq hundreds of times. He could have reenacted both scenes from everyone's vantage point.

But it was his Russian hosts who had opened up the most useful memory. The day Nasser came to them, Nonna had spoken to her husband in Russian. The words had sounded familiar to Nasser. In his overwhelmed state, he had assumed it was just a sound of comfort his spirit recognized and wanted.

Nasser stayed on with his friends, helping Anastasii

restore his back garden with his young sons. Since Nasser knew only a few words of Russian, Anastasii often translated for him into English—the language they had spoken at work.

One evening over family dinner, Anastasii's boys argued about where they wanted to travel that coming summer. Anastasii replied in Russian and sighed. The sound of one of his words clicked in Nasser's subconscious: He immediately thought of General Nikolayev and what Nonna had said the day he arrived.

Nasser asked, "What did you say?"

Anastasii sighed again. "That they don't know what it is to want a vacation."

"That last word—can you repeat it in Russian?"

Anastasii raised an eyebrow but complied. Nasser's memory expanded.

He stared beyond his bowl of borscht. The word was one Nasser had heard the night he eavesdropped. It was one of the words the general had said in Russian as he stormed out of the burned building—a word spoken in the same sentence as the Dead Sea.

Eventually, Nasser pieced together that the general was planning some kind of vacation on the Dead Sea in a matter of weeks.

It had taken Nasser that intervening time and several risky assignations to find out where. And now he was there—the hotel where General Nikolayev and several other Russians were registered.

And either the general didn't eat breakfast, or he had ordered room service. Nasser scanned through the Haaretz again.

He started to read one of the articles, and he almost dropped the paper. A woman had written about the Overcomers. Shafiq's people. Hungry for more, Nasser read the entire piece, forgetting to keep an eye on the lobby passersby. That now-familiar spirit sense rose through him. He wanted whatever it was.

Nasser closed his eyes. He wasn't sure if he was praying, but he was certainly asking.

When he opened his eyes, he saw the general and several other men coming from the elevators. Nasser had been researching photos of the Russian. In them, he had seen many other government officials. It seemed the general liked to vacation with his colleagues. That, or this wasn't a vacation.

Nasser watched them head for the outdoor pool. After a short pause, he followed with a towel and his new smart phone set to microphone.

Once again, Nasser hoped to have some news for his friend Shafiq.

FORT WORTH, TEXAS

Jesse Mae grabbed the remote control from Della and hit the volume up four times, smearing the buttons with bacon grease. The news anchor, her polished hair immobile, explained the slow motion images of the bomb that had been captured on a tourist's cell phone.

Over the bursting stone and dust, the woman announced the event that had usurped all others during Israel's Independence Day celebrations. "A suicide bomb, set off by a newly identified Russian-Iranian terrorist group, was prevented from the fullest extent of its intended damage by an Arabic man who seemed to be trying to protect a Jewish boy from the blast—this according to eyewitnesses.

"Authorities confirmed that all three men died, in addition to the immediate passersby, but that the force of the explosion had been lessened by the Arabic man, now identified as Jalil Mahfouz.

"The bomber's identify is still being established. The boy's name has not yet been released, though it has been confirmed that he is a U.S. citizen."

Jesse Mae looked across the breakfast nook at Della, who still held her coffee mid-air, forgotten. She set down the mug and looked at her friend.

The news anchor continued. "But some good news out of Israel. The unparalleled success of the Havilah Gas Fields has sent EIS stock soaring. Investors say..." Della clicked off the television.

Jesse Mae closed her eyes and began mumbling a semi-inaudible prayer. Della caught only two words before beginning her own: resurrection life.

Chapter Forty-two
Jerusalem, Israel

THE MAGEN DAVID Adom—Israel's version of the Red Cross—arrived within minutes of the police. Medical techs hopped out of the vans and instantly began treating the victims.

Ma'ayan kept feeling for a pulse in Eitan's neck. Nothing.

"Come back, come back!" She had pulled the white scarf from her shoulders and used it to staunch the blood that wouldn't stop running from Eitan's torso.

Ma'ayan wasn't aware of anyone or anything but the body of her son lying on the stones, his eyes open but unseeing.

"Come back!"

Sirens. Dust in her eyes. Her knees vaguely in pain.

Someone calling her name, "Eitan?" No—his lips hadn't moved.

She heard it again, then saw Shafiq kneeling beside her, bringing a man with a medical bag who knelt on the other side of her son.

Miriam sat in shock, still as a stone, at Eitan's feet. Her face was blanched white except for a smear of dust and a trickle of blood.

The man felt through Eitan's bloody chest to where his heart had once beat.

The past tense started to creep through Ma'ayan's heart. Once. Had. She shook her head as hard as she could to shake out that thought.

"Now! Come back, now!"

Beyond the urgency of the moment, Ma'ayan felt an anger rise within her. It shot through her, massive and immediate. Just as it increased to the point where she could no longer contain it, she felt another part of herself offer peace—peace to her anger and peace to the one or ones who had caused this destruction.

As she clutched her son's hands with her now bloodied fingers, a swell of imagery rose and fell across her heart: Morgan kneeling in front of Peter's mother asking her forgiveness for an act he did not commit. Tito blessing those who had killed the woman he loved. Della draping her guests in white scarves at the wake.

Ma'ayan looked down at the white scarf now sopping red.

A possibility presented itself in this, her fullest knowing of loss in her life: She could continue forward in her anger or release it before it took up residence within her.

The anger within asked, "How will you fight without me on your side?

The peace asked, "Do you trust me to fight for you?"

The medical technician lay his hand on Eitan's chest and looked at Ma'ayan. In English, he said, "I'm sorry. He is gone. There is nothing we can do."

"Nothing?" Ma'ayan looked at Shafiq as the medical tech left for another fallen victim.

With her arms, she gathered her son up to her chest. With her spirit, she yanked on Shafiq's own spirit. Her eyes found his over the top of her son's head.

She begged him with every facet of her being. "Don't leave me with nothing."

FORT WORTH, TEXAS

Karla Wexler laid her hand on her friend's arm. "Sasha, dear, will you excuse me for a moment? Something vital just came up."

Sasha, teacup suspended in mid-air, watched her friend walk out of the drawing room. She looked around—no one stood in the doorway. No phone had rung. What vital thing had happened without her noticing?

While sipping tea with her friend, Karla had felt the distinct impression that she needed to pray for a circumstance in Israel. She passed through the great hall and up the stairs. She stepped into the small room at the back of the house with a balcony overlooking the garden. This was her prayer room, her sanctuary. She had created it, inspired by the scriptural description of Solomon's palace, to get away with God. When Solomon sought out God's wisdom, he ascended the stairs of his palace and listened for advice—even in the middle of a dinner party with the Queen of Sheba. If the Queen of Sheba could wait a minute, so could Sasha, the charity's chairwoman.

Karla stood in front of her French doors, looking down into the gravel walkways lined with bluebonnets and white lilies. The unction came: She was to pray for someone's destiny—destiny that was in the process of being thwarted.

"I call on heaven's best for this circumstance. I speak against the powers of darkness, that they give way to the power of light. I speak life to areas of death. And I call forth those nearby to walk in the power you have given them."

Chapter Forty-three

Tel Aviv, Israel

IYA'S HOUSE FELT empty to her. She hadn't had a morning alone since the arrival of her granddaughter and great-grandson, and she'd loved it. She was surprised. She'd lived alone for so long she thought she'd grown used to the solitude. She poured herself a glass of mint tea and walked out to the front garden. It was midday, and the heat told her summer was coming. As she turned to go back inside, she saw the newspaper. She'd forgotten it in the rush of getting the kids out of the house and on their way to Jerusalem.

She picked it up and smiled: Ma'ayan had said her article would appear today. The Haaretz in one hand and her glass in the other, Liya made her way to the bench near the garden door to Ma'ayan's room and sat in the shade.

Liya always loved to see and read her granddaughter's work. She told her friends she kept her English going just for that pleasure.

Liya opened the paper and smiled when she found the name Ma'ayan Bracha. There she was: her granddaughter in an Israeli paper! And writing about the Overcomers! Liya hugged the paper to her chest, blinking back tears. Her prayers of all these years had been answered. Her granddaughter was walking in her destiny—and with her feet in her homeland.

Liya released the paper and began reading about the group that had become part of her own life, her extended

family: the Overcomers. Ma'ayan started off with stories—
like she always did. She told of confirmed reports of healings, miracles, and operations that no natural mind could
solve, but that these empowered people had facilitated
because of their ability to walk in supernatural power.
She told about their honor and not taking credit for any
of these things. She told of the insight the Overcomers
received through unusual acts of prayer and intercession.

She told of the white stones they wore and why: how
each Overcomer received a new name when they received
their white stone. This new name symbolized their fullest
identity in the God they served, as was the case in both
the Tanakh and New Testament: Abram was renamed
Abraham, Jacob was renamed Israel, Saul was renamed
Paul.

She told of rumors of people being raised from the
dead—being given new life. And even if that was just a
metaphorical new life—like that of a new name—was
there perhaps power in that new name?

Ma'ayan ended her article with a question for her readers,
"If, as these people claim, we can all be Overcomers, what
would your name be?"

Liya wasn't the only one who asked herself that question. Like her, thousands and thousands of Israelis had
been reading about the supernatural group in homes from
Golan Heights to the Red Sea. Muslims and Jews and
Christians alike.

What neither Ma'ayan nor Liya knew was that just by
reading about a realm of possibility within their reach, the
spirit eyes of even skeptical readers were opening around
the country. And since early that morning, their questions
had been received as prayers.

JERUSALEM, ISRAEL

Ma'ayan was looking at Shafiq with a look that could pull heaven to earth. She was still hugging her son close to her torso.

Shafiq felt the pull of a parent's love for her child. As he did, he felt the divine Father's love for His Son. The power of this perfect love extended from Shafiq's heart. This is where it would begin.

To Ma'ayan, he said, "Put on the necklace your friend gave you. And trust me."

Then he gently took Eitan from Ma'ayan and stood with him, clasping the body in an upright position. Shakily, Ma'ayan stood as well. Shafiq felt the weight of the young man he knew had a greater destiny than death.

Looking worried but willing, Ma'ayan held her son's head upright.

Shafiq turned to her, "Your new spirit name is Hannah. It means favor and grace. You receive favor, and it is time for you to extend grace. Forgive him."

Ma'ayan knew who Shafiq meant. Her heart had already told her as much. She nodded, "I forgive."

Shafiq turned back to Eitan. Eye to lifeless eye, Shafiq looked into the dead boy's face. "I breathe ruach breath into you, divine life. I call forth the leader I saw when you first arrived to this country. I call forth the children you will bring into this world to bring it peace. I call forth all life that brings forth life. Return!" And then he exhaled loudly into the dead young man's face.

To Ma'ayan, Shafiq said, "Put your hand on his mouth and nose."

Ma'ayan did so. She held her breath even as she felt something on her palm—the palm resting on her son's face. Through the shellac of dried blood on her skin, she thought she felt his—

"Breath! I feel his breath! Eitan!"

Her son's still-open eyes blinked.

ELSEWHERE

In Fort Worth, the bluebells waved from their garden beds in the wind. Mrs. Wexler nodded and turned to descend her stairs and find her husband.

Jesse Mae and Della started dancing in Della's living room, sloshing their coffee and making up song lyrics that rhymed with "alive." Jive. Revive. Arrive.

Tito Marnina kissed the rose before laying it on Nikki's grave and said, "Forgive me."

In Tel Aviv, Ishay said into his phone, "Yes, I'll let her know."

Liya closed the paper and rose to get the phone before it rang.

Near a pool by the Dead Sea, Nasser pocketed his smart phone and turned in the direction the Russians had left, praying Anastasii could translate something from the recording to help the Overcomers.

Offshore on the drilling platform, Zadok walked among the fallen streamers and sunken balloons that littered the staff cafeteria from the previous evening's Independence celebration. He pulled a single, white balloon by its string and walked out to the railing. The wind yanked at his hair and the fragile white orb. Zadok held it to the sky and said, "We have overcome."

The sky accepted the balloon with quick thanks, taking it into invisible but real heights.

Chapter Forty-four

From "Spine of Faith," by Ma'ayan Bracha

A S WITH ANY faith-based agency, there is plenty that can't be explained in black and white. Perhaps the best explanation of the OTF's seemingly super-human abilities comes from the Overcomers themselves. To protect those whose positions would be compromised, the OTF quoted below are identified by their job title:

Linguist: Most people think wrong. They think that if they follow five simple steps in a precise order—like turning the combination to a safe—they can obtain access to success or status or whatever. They think turning that combination will open up something inside them. But that something is already inside them. The only formula you need is faith. And that faith path will look different for everyone.

Drill Sergeant: What makes the OTF different? We are prepared to solve things others can't because we ask heaven for insight. We ask for divine appointments. Visions. Knowledge. You name it—you ask for it—you got it.

Professor of Quantum Physics: Are we here? Yes. Are we somewhere else? Yes. We live in an intersection of time-lines. Heaven intersecting with earth. Constantly, these two realities collide. But we usually limit our vision to the earthly one—and only notice the heavenly one when the collision is particularly great. When heaven collides with earth, it passes through the atmospheric realm where the enemy lives. He likes to mess up the plans of heaven, and

when he tries, it can get messy. We can feel the shaking.
My dear, late colleague, Professor Uziel, knew that the two
timelines were converging: it was and it will be again—
heaven on earth. Heaven is working backwards through
time, invading earth, and earth is pressing forward. We
are all playing out the invasion. But some of us know it,
and some of us don't.

Rabbi: Only when you know something exists in the
supernatural can you help establish it in the natural realm.
The power to demonstrate God's will flows through the
knower. Your knower puts a demand on what is unseen.
In other words, the measure of your doing is determined
by the measure of your knowing. You can't do what you
don't know.

Special Ops: All I have to say is: I wish an Acts 9 experience on whoever reads this. That'll change everything.
And I bless you with an Ananias to help you figure it out.

Special Ops: "As we walk in the prophetic purpose of
God, we can become 'invincible' until we finish the work
He has for us. This is our argument with death. We are
here until our assignment is finished.

JERUSALEM, ISRAEL

Shafiq gave one of his rare smiles. Eitan was standing
for the first time since the bombing. The doctors hadn't
believed he would be out of bed for months. But they also
hadn't believed he had been raised from the dead.

Eitan smiled back at Shafiq. Despite his crinkled hos-
pital gown and multiple bandages, Eitan looked hale and
hearty. His spirit shone through his eyes in a different way.
Ma'ayan caught herself staring at him—this new Eitan.
The one who had touched heaven.

With Shafiq spotting him on one side and Ma'ayan on

the other, Eitan took measured steps away from the bed he'd spent the last few days in.

"Everything works!" Eitan said, laughing.

There it was again; even his voice seemed different. More confident? No—he'd always been that. This was more like joy had taken up residence in Eitan. A strong, sure, and constant joy.

Eitan pivoted and turned back toward the bed. "I can predict that the doctor will tell me that's enough for now."

Shafiq helped him back on the bed.

Eitan lay back on his pillow and said, "Ranan."

Ma'ayan asked, "Did Miriam teach you that word?"

"No, it was given to me."

Shafiq looked at Ma'ayan, who looked back at her son. "Given?"

"When I went there. 'Ranan' is a cry of joy. It's what I heard as I returned here. But it also means 'to overcome.' 'To be overcome with joy.'"

Something tingled in Ma'ayan's spirit. She asked, "Why did you start walking toward the man with the bomb?"

Eitan smiled at her—not just with his mouth; his entire being smiled at her. "I heard the ranan. I knew what it was as I heard it; it's the power of joy—Overcomer joy. And I knew that man was trying to stop it. He couldn't of course. No one can. It is the jubilation word for the God of the chosen ones. It's what I came back for. To help people hear it."

The doctor returned in time to hear this and suggested Eiten rest. He told Ma'ayan. "Go out. Get some fresh air."

She nodded and Shafiq walked with her out of the Shaare Zekek Medical Center where Ma'ayan had spent most of the last few days.

Ma'ayan realized Shafiq was still with her. "I'm going for a walk. Would you like to come?"

Shafiq answered by following. Though the two were silent, the traffic of the Sderot Herzl highway was loud. They crossed toward Mount Herzl Memorial Park on the other side. The late afternoon was warm, the sky full of heat.

At the drab, mid-century entrance to the memorial, Ma'ayan paused a moment before stepping through the gates. Her son had almost ended up in a cemetery. She wondered for a moment: would she have buried him here or taken him back to Texas? She entered the grounds, thinking of Fort Worth, of her life there with her son. What kind of life was it for either of them?

Ma'ayan and Shafiq wandered beneath the cedars of Lebanan and pine trees, through the pale stone graves with their green beds. They arrived to the flower-encircled memorial of Theodor Herzl.

Ma'ayan stopped and finally spoke. "Here lies a journalist who changed the world."

"He won't be the last."

Ma'ayan smiled. "I don't know about me. But maybe I can…through Eitan. Maybe through him."

A breeze shook the flowers around the dark, square marker engraved with the visionary's name in gold. On top of the maker lay a collection of small stones, left there by visitors. Beyond the memorial, lay the collection of stone buildings of Jerusalem left there by history. The holy city glowed in western light. It seemed to promise not just a past but a future.

Ma'ayan reached for Shafiq's hand. It was already open, waiting. She looked at him. "I will stay here. My son and I—we will stay."

•ך•

The necklace was expanding from her throat, the white stone pendant giving her new name a voice of authority. This time, she felt the necklace not as constriction but as expansion. She was finally ready to wear it. She was ready to step into her identity.

She leaned back her head, shouting with ranan, "It is mine!"

Laughing, Ma'ayan sat up straight in bed.

It wasn't a dream. She was wearing the necklace. And she had heaven on earth.

EPILOGUE

*Look at the nations and watch—and be utterly
amazed. For I am going to do something in your days
that you would not believe, even if you were told.*
—HABAKKUK 1:5

THE UNIVERSITY WAS buzzing with end-of-year energy. Students crossed the green spaces in various diagonal lines. Two young men stood still among them, just outside of the building that housed the school of computer science. One was tall and dark, the other of medium build with reddish hair.

The dark-haired man turned to the other and said, "Thank you. I think I will."

His new friend smiled. "Good. I look forward to it. Hey. Your story about the vav—did you know that it's also the Hebrew word for 'and'? It is the ultimate connector. I even named my last program after it."

The other man smiled. "Yes. I lived that connection."

A phone rang, both men fumbled for their pockets. The dark-haired man found that it was his. He glanced at the number and his face tightened. To his friend, he said, "I think this is the call I mentioned I was waiting for. I have to take it. I'll see you soon."

The red-haired man nodded and waved before turning back inside the building.

"Hello?"

A palm tree snapped its fronds in the wind.

The young man smiled. "I would be happy to speak with the president."

213